Torrie's Hero

The viscount turned to face her, his lips thinned in anger. "I don't know what kind of game you are playing, Lady Victoria, but I refuse to take part."

"It's no game. It's my life, my future. I made a vow, you see."

"To whom? If this is between you and the Almighty, I swear I have not been in His good graces for years. I doubt He even recalls my existence."

Torrie was not about to get into a discussion of faith and fallen sparrows. "To the Fates, then. Or to myself. I promised that if I was saved, I would wed, to make my parents happy and to fulfill my destiny. . . . I asked for a favor and you arrived."

"You were not making a bargain with your Maker, then—you were making a deal with the devil." He held his arms out. "Look at what such a foolish barter brought you. You should have negotiated better terms, if you were wagering your soul."

The
Diamond Key

Barbara Metzger

A SIGNET BOOK

SIGNET
Published by New American Library, a division of
Penguin Putnam Inc., 375 Hudson Street,
New York, New York 10014, U.S.A.
Penguin Books Ltd, 80 Strand,
London WC2R 0RL, England
Penguin Books Australia Ltd, 250 Camberwell Road,
Camberwell, Victoria 3124, Australia
Penguin Books Canada Ltd, 10 Alcorn Avenue,
Toronto, Ontario, Canada M4V 3B2
Penguin Books (N.Z.) Ltd, Cnr Rosedale and Airborne Roads,
Albany, Auckland 1310, New Zealand

Penguin Books Ltd, Registered Offices:
Harmondsworth, Middlesex, England

First published by Signet, an imprint of New American Library,
a division of Penguin Putnam Inc.

First Printing, April 2003
10 9 8 7 6 5 4 3 2 1

To all the WTC heroes,
including the rescue dogs

Chapter One

First came the smoke. Then came the heat. Last were the screams from the front of Madame Michaela's dressmaking shop.

"Fire! Fire! Get out!"

"Lawks a'mercy," came from the mantua-maker herself, her fake French accent melting away with the silks and satins, ribbons and lace. "M'bloody shop! Help!"

Torrie, Lady Victoria Ann Keyes, stood frozen for a moment atop the pedestal in the fitting room where *madame*'s assistant was measuring her against the sections of already cut green velvet. "Go," Lady Torrie told the wide-eyed young girl. "Tina, is it? Go find out what is happening. Quickly now."

Tina dropped her pins and her tape and pieces of what was to be Torrie's new riding habit, and fled the little back room.

The screams grew louder, the smoke thicker. Tina was not coming back, obviously, and Torrie could not wait another second. Unfortunately, she stood on the raised platform in her shift and stockings, while her gown and shoes were on a stool in a corner, obscured now by the billows of black. Torrie grabbed up a piece of green velvet—though what good a sleeve was going to do to protect her modesty, she frantically wondered—and headed barefooted toward Madame Michaela's shrieking voice. Then she remembered her maid.

Ruthie Cobb had been feeling poorly, likely with the

same enervating ague affecting Torrie's mother, so Torrie had asked the modiste if Ruthie could rest somewhere during the fitting. Loath to offend one of her best clients, Madame Michaela had herself shown Ruthie to a cot in one of the rear storage rooms. What if the abigail were asleep, not hearing the cries to leave the building? Torrie changed direction and raced down the back hall, hopping on one foot when a pin pierced her heel.

The smoke was now coming from this end of the shop, too, but Torrie ran on, past a deserted cutting room, calling to her maid. She heard nothing back but the roar of a fire. But there! There was the storage room, fabrics piled to the ceiling, and the empty cot, thank goodness. Torrie could leave.

Smoke was pouring in from where the rear door should have been, though, and flames were already snaking from the front of the shop toward the cutting room, where the bits and pieces of fabric on the floor would ignite to an inferno. Trying not to let panic overcome her judgment, Torrie spun around and spotted a high window. There, if she could just reach it, she'd be through and in the alley before her situation became desperate. She dragged the wooden cot over and stood on it, able to reach the latch and push open the window, but she was simply not tall enough to hoist herself so high. Bolts of fabric would do the trick. She pulled one, heavier than she thought it would be, off a shelf, then another, dragging them toward the bed, trying to keep them stacked securely. A third went on top. Gasping from the smoke and the effort and the rising fear, she climbed up—and the whole structure collapsed around her: the bolts, the bed, and the broken window frame. Falling, she grabbed for the nearest handhold, but only dislodged more fabric rolls from another pile. The entire mass came down, then the rack that was leaning on it, then two neighboring shelves. On Torrie.

With strength she did not know she possessed, ignoring the pain in her head where she must have hit it against the wall or the floor, Torrie started shoving the bolts off her, rolling them away until she could sit up. She could get no farther, though, for her foot was trapped beneath the broken bed, which was beneath a mound of now-unfurled fabrics that she could not reach to push aside.

She was going to die. Lady Victoria Ann Keyes, daughter of an earl, darling of society, diamond of the first water, was going to die amid unsold dress lengths. She was already coughing, her lungs straining for clean air. Tears flowed down her cheeks, and not just from the smoke irritating her eyes. She was too young to die. Why, at twenty years of age, she had barely begun to live!

Not ready to give up, Torrie twisted around until she could move one more bolt of brocade, one more length of linsey-woolsey, another spool of sarcenet. Then she heard the bells. No angels welcoming her to the hereafter, these were the fire bells, the whistles and shouts of the fire brigade. Madame Michaela had paid her insurance, thank goodness. Help was on its way. Torrie shouted, "Here! I am here in the back!"

Fires make a great deal of noise, she found. So did the firefighters, clearing the streets, dragging their hose, ordering bucket lines. It would be a miracle if anyone heard her in time.

Well, if a miracle was what it was going to take to get her out of this hell, Torrie decided, she'd start praying. The problem was, aside from the heat and the smoke and the mounds of material on top of her, Torrie did not know any but the prayers she recited every Sunday. This was not the time for rote words. Neither, it occurred to her, was it the time for asking for favors, when she had not been on such terms with the Almighty before. She had even missed church a few Sundays, after dancing until nearly dawn the evenings before. And she had definitely taken the Lord's name in vain—just before, when she'd stepped on that pin. She had never committed murder or stolen anything, of course, but she had frequently gossiped, and last week she had definitely coveted Lady Valentine's Italianate garden with its marble piazza. No, she had not been a very righteous, religious person, so why should anyone answer her prayers?

She was not a very good daughter, either, Torrie sadly reflected. Honor her parents? Why, they only wished her happiness in a secure future. Had she given them their dearest wish? No. After three Seasons she was still unwed, and Mama and Papa were still without grandchildren, still dragging themselves to London for the social rounds. Papa missed his sheep, and Mama missed her gardens, yet they persisted, so their beloved only child might find the man of her dreams.

Torrie clutched at the charm she wore on a gold chain around her neck, a gold key set with diamonds. Her father had presented it to her the evening of her comeout ball when she was seventeen.

"Now, go find the heart this key unlocks, poppet," Papa had said, beaming with pride between his beautiful young daughter and the beautiful countess who still held the key to his own heart.

Torrie had never found that matching piece of herself, although she'd had offers aplenty. Flowers were tossed at her feet, compliments were thrown at her head, rings were pressed on her fingers, but nary a heart was opened to her, at least none that made her own beat faster. Lord Skyler had no prospects but a rich wife's dowry, even if he would be a duke one day. Sir Stanley followed his own muse, spouting dreadful poetry, and Mr. Drosher drooled. Those were only the most recent offers for her hand—and for her father's wealth.

Look where her fussy, finicky heart had led her, though, to breathe her last in a burning building, alone and unloved. Torrie swore then and there to change her ways if her life was spared. She'd marry the next man her father dragged home from White's, someone stolid and stable, just like Papa. Only let her live, she vowed, and she'd wed the next man who asked, fop, fool, or fortune hunter. No, she decided, she'd marry the man who rescued her. He might be a sausage-smelling, ale-swilling employee of the insurance company, but no matter. With her monies, he could buy his own fire protection agency. The *beau monde* would be closed to Lady Victoria Ann Keyes and her lowborn spouse, but Torrie had had her fill of balls and routs. She'd settle for a country cottage, a cradle to rock, and a caring husband. Just let him hurry, she prayed. Just in case no one was listening to silent prayers this horrible afternoon, Torrie yelled as loudly as she could. "Help! Please help!"

Wynn Ingram, Viscount Ingall, was walking down the street, deep in thought, letting his dog choose the way. He barely heard the commotion of the fire wagons and the rushing crowds, so lost was he in his dismal reflections. When someone shouted at him to get out of the way, he finally took note of his surroundings. Unwilling to join the spectators lined up to watch a building burn down—and peoples' lives put at risk—Wynn turned back the way he had come. His damn fool of a dog, though, ran down the alley, barking his stupid head off, headed straight for the conflagration. The curly-coated terrier had adopted Wynn when the viscount's Bombay clipper had pulled into port, and no amount of curses or threats had discouraged the clunch. Since the mutton-headed mongrel was the only one to welcome Wynn back to England after six years, Lord Ingall had relented. The dog had not left his side since. Such loyalty counted for something to a man who had known so little of it, so Wynn followed the little dog down the alley.

"Help! Please help!" he heard over the babel and bells and barking.

"Bloody hell," he cursed, but ran farther down the alley, searching for a back entrance to the burning shop. A trash barrel was blocking the rear door, and he cursed again at the jackass who would leave it there, trapping those within. Then he saw that the barrel was on fire, too, with flames licking at the building's back wall. With no thought for himself, he shoved the barrel aside and crashed through the door, the dunderheaded dog on his heels. Wynn tried to shield his mouth and nose from the smoke as he stumbled through a workroom and down a dark corridor. The cries for help had stopped, damn it, but he followed the dog's high-pitched yips.

The terrier was frantically digging at a mound of fabric. No, Wynn could just distinguish a woman buried under the pile. He pushed the dog aside and started hurling bolts of fabric, then wood, until she was free. Wynn could not tell if she was still breathing, but he could see she was nearly naked. He cursed again. Coughing, he took his coat off to wrap her in, not to protect her modesty, but to protect the pale white skin that gleamed even through the near pitch-black smoke.

"Do not die now, damn you," he yelled, gathering her up and making a mad dash back the way he had come, through smoke and flames and finally oilskin-coated men with buckets and hoses. He kept running, ignoring her slight weight, intent only on finding fresh air and help for the poor woman.

He paused a moment, looking for a safe place to lay her down. Then he heard the most welcome sound of his life: a deep rasping breath. The female was alive, thank heaven. He carried her still farther from the fire.

The woman gasped and choked and gasped again. Then she managed to ask in a hoarse whisper, "Are you married?"

Wynn almost dropped her. "Hell, no."

"Good," she croaked. "Then you can marry me. I made a vow, you see, to wed my savior."

The viscount looked down to make sure his dog was still following. "It was Homer who saved your life, ma'am."

Just before she lost consciousness again, Torrie rasped out: "Oh, is he married?"

Chapter Two

The street around the fire scene was a bedlam, which was where Wynn's burden belonged. No, he corrected himself, she had merely breathed in too much smoke. Her brain was befogged. Normally, he guessed, she was as rational as any woman ever was. The sooner she was in the care of a physician, the better for both of them, no matter how trustingly she wrapped her arm around his neck and pressed herself against his chest.

Wynn might take in a homeless, hungry dog, but a woman, a well-formed, well-bred woman at that? Hell, no. The viscount could not judge her looks, not under the soot and the streaks, but he guessed she'd be blond, from that fair skin he'd glimpsed. He'd wager she was beautiful, too, the last thing he needed in his life.

"Come on, Homer. Someone is bound to be looking for the lady."

Someone was. An overdressed, under-chinned man ran up to them. "Lady Torrie, thank goodness." He wiped his brow with a lace-edged handkerchief, which he then tucked up his sleeve before holding out his arms. "Here, man, I'll take her."

The fellow's bottle-green coat was stretched so tightly across his narrow shoulders that the seams would likely split if he carried anything heavier than his hat.

"Nonsense," Wynn told him. "I have her. Just find a carriage to take the lady home."

The man chewed on the knuckles of his yellow Limerick gloves in indecision. "My coach is around the corner. But I . . . But you . . ."

"Go on, man. Lead the way."

The foppish gentleman still hesitated, obviously reluctant to leave the lady in a stranger's care. Wynn could hardly blame him, knowing he must look like a Barbary Coast pirate, with his coat off, his neckcloth undone, and his face most likely as filthy as the female's. "This is no time for the social niceties. Lady—Torrie, you say?— needs a doctor's care."

"Lady Victoria Ann Keyes," the smaller man pronounced in near reverence. "Daughter of Earl Duchamp."

The names meant nothing to Wynn, so long had he been out of the country. Besides, his arms were getting tired, now that he was standing still. Impatient, he snapped, "Well, the earl will be frantic to get his daughter back if he gets word of the fire, so either lead us to your carriage or get out of the way."

The dandified chap scurried ahead, his walking stick tucked under his arm. Wynn followed, Homer barked, and the woman groaned. "Not much longer, my lady," Wynn murmured soothingly. "Perhaps your friend has something to drink in his carriage. Your throat must be parched." Wynn's was, and he had not been in the smoke half as long. He doubted the green-clad gossoon had anything as practical as a flask. A mirror and comb were more likely.

Wynn debated finding a glass of water for her. "How much longer?" he asked.

The smaller man was stopped at a green-and-gold carriage with a crest on the door. "Right here. I'll take her now."

"No, you give the driver her address, then run ahead"—he amended that, noting the fellow's spindly legs and highly polished pumps—"no, hire a boy to run or ride ahead to alert her household. She needs cold drinks, a bath, and a physician waiting."

The man stood by the open carriage door, his prominent eyes fixed on Lady Victoria as if she were made of spun sugar and about to melt. He gnawed on his fingers again, without stepping aside. "But I was to be the one . . . That is, I should carry her home. Lady Torrie's intended, don't you know."

The woman raised her head from Wynn's shoulder and coughed to clear her throat. "Fustian, Boyce. You intend to pay your debts with my dowry, is all. Besides, I am going to marry this gentleman. I vowed I would."

Wynn would have thrust the smoke-stunned female into Lord Boyce's puny embrace before she could say Jack Robinson, but the jackanapes was reaching for the ribbon of his quizzing glass. "You cannot marry a lowly fireman, Torrie. It ain't done." Then he had the glass in place and squinted through it. "Egad, it's Ingram."

"Viscount Ingall now," Wynn corrected him, finally recognizing George St. Brenner from his early school days, aeons ago, it seemed. He nodded his head slightly in acknowledgment of the acquaintance, and of the other man's ascension to his own family honors. "Lord Boyce."

"Great Heavens, Torrie, the dastard is worse than a bucket bearer. He's barred from society, exiled from the country, even. Marry him? Why, you cannot be seen with such a scoundrel, much less let him carry you home. His reputation—"

"My reputation be hanged," Wynn said, stepping around Boyce. "The lady needs care."

"But . . . but . . ."

Wynn was already stepping up into the coach, his weight combined with the woman in his arms making the carriage sway. He held her more tightly. Instead of placing her on the squabs, he sat with her in his lap. She'd fall off the seat, otherwise, Wynn told himself.

The dog jumped in after them, then turned and showed his teeth to Lord Boyce, whose mouth hung open. He was still staring through his quizzing glass.

"But . . . but . . ." he stammered, "she cannot go with you!"

Freeing one hand, Wynn rapped on the roof of the coach, signaling the driver to start. "Go on, Boyce. The lady is safe with me."

As the carriage moved forward, Torrie pulled her other arm—the one that was not wrapped around her rescuer's neck—from his enveloping coat and softly patted his cheek. "Of course I am safe with you. You already saved my life. That is why we have to get married."

"Maybe Boyce has a flask in here after all," the viscount declared, immediately shoving the woman onto the opposing seat, next to the dog, so he could search. At least one of them desperately needed a drink.

Marry her? Hell, he'd already lost his honor, given up six years of his life away from his homeland, and forfeited the respect of his family, all for a woman. He'd be damned if he was going to sacrifice his freedom for another flea-brained female.

Wynn Ingram, Viscount Ingall, did not trust women.

He did not like women.

He sure as Hades did not understand women.

What seemed to be fifteen females threw themselves at Wynn the moment he crossed the open threshold of Duchamp House in Grosvenor Square. Wynn never thought he would have missed the Canadian wilderness.

There were white-faced maids, one hand-wringing abigail who swore the whole disaster was her fault, and an anxious housekeeper waiting for instructions. One woman cried, "My baby!" and had to be supported closer by a black-clad female so she could see for herself that Lady Victoria still breathed, and brushed a strand of begrimed hair off her cheek.

"I am fine, Mama, truly." Torrie's voice was low and raspy, but strong. "This fine gentleman rescued me in time."

A damp-eyed butler took over then, snapping his fingers for two stalwart footmen to remove Wynn's burden; another flick of his hand had two of the maids hurrying ahead while the menservants carefully bore their fragile cargo up the marble arched stairs.

A female who had to be Lady Duchamp turned on the steps to address Wynn, whose arms felt oddly empty. "Please stay so I may thank you properly, as soon as I have seen to Torrie. And my husband has been sent for. He'll wish to—"

"Please do not concern yourself, my lady. Your daughter's well-being is reward enough."

"No, you must stay. I insist."

Wynn recognized the same implacable air of authority and the same determined chin he'd noted in Lady Victoria. If the daughter resembled her mother in other ways, he considered, the girl was indeed an exquisite. Countess Duchamp was an elegant, graceful woman with reddish hair under a scrap of lace. She barely seemed old enough to be the mother of a marriageable chit. He choked on the mental mention of the word marriage, and Lady Duchamp pounced on the sound.

"There. You need a restorative. I should have offered sooner."

"No, ma'am. I would not wish to be in the way at this time of great concern."

"I will not hear of your leaving, and that is the end of it. Lady Ann, my sister-in-law, can look to your needs while I see to Torrie." She nodded toward the frowning, black-gowned female who remained in the hall near Wynn, as if checking to make certain he did not make off with any of the silver. The aunt's glare was so chilling, Wynn could feel his spine shivering. He never thought he'd miss the heat of Bombay, either. If Lady Torrie resembled this old dragon, it was no wonder she was unwed. Before Wynn could make a dash toward the front door, Lady Duchamp concluded: "Besides, you will have to wait for your coat."

Wynn did not fancy traipsing through London in his shirtsleeves, in fact, nor walking back to his lodgings in Kensington. Boyce's carriage had driven off, and Wynn would never ask to borrow a Duchamp coach. He could not hire a hackney, though, not while his purse was in the pocket of his jacket, which was even then disappearing around a corner, still wrapped around Lady Torrie. One of the maids was tucking a blanket around her, but not before he caught a glimpse of one dainty ankle.

The aunt cleared her throat and scowled at him, making him feel like a spotty-faced youth caught with his hand up a milkmaid's skirts. "Perhaps a dish of water for my dog, then," was all he could think to say.

Lady Ann sniffed and led the way down the hall to an opulent white-and-gold parlor. She gestured toward a tray of decanters and glasses while she gave orders to the butler, but Wynn did not stray from the entrance to the lavishly decorated room. In his present filthy state he was not fit for the intricately carved moldings, painted ceiling, and priceless works of art in every niche. In fact, he did not belong in any part of this magnificent home, and never would no matter how he was dressed. As soon as Lady Duchamp realized who he was, or her husband the earl returned, they'd be glad to see the back of Wynn Ingram quickly enough. He ought to leave before they were forced to be polite to such a pariah. He could wash up in the kitchens and perhaps have a glass of ale.

It was too late, for Homer was lapping at a crystal dish a servant had set on the floor. The little dog barely looked civilized on his best days, and this was not one of those. He appeared more black than his usual tan, and bits of cinder and strands of thread were matted onto his short curly coat. One side of his mustache must have been singed off, leaving him lopsided and more vagabondish than the viscount himself. At least Wynn did not slosh his drink on the fine Turkey carpet.

"I should leave," Wynn told Lady Ann, who was still frowning her disapproval. Most likely her face was frozen that way, he decided. "I doubt my coat can be worn again, anyway."

She was holding out a dampened cloth. "Did you really rescue my niece from the fire?"

He nodded yes. "But it was Homer who heard her calls and led me to her."

Instead of handing Wynn the linen, the earl's sister bent and started wiping at the dog. "I love my niece," the dragon murmured, dampening Homer more with her tears than the towel. "She bears my name as her middle one. Thank you."

Homer wagged his tail and went back to the water dish.

Lud, now Wynn was alone with a starched-up female who was old enough to be his mother—except his mother had never cried over him, not even when he left England, never to see her again. Wynn hoped Lady Torrie appreciated what she had: so many people to care about her welfare, to worry about her, to love her.

He had his dog.

Chapter Three

"Torrie? Where is my girl?"

Wynn could hear the frantic calls even through the thick oak door of the parlor.

The earl had returned from his club, having received the news of a fire. As Lord Duchamp pounded up the stairs, Wynn could hear him calling to his wife, "Maggie, where are you?" And to the butler, "Mallen, she is all right, isn't she? Tell me my little girl is all right."

Again, Wynn felt that wrench on his heartstrings at the love in this family.

"I'll be leaving now," he told Lady Ann. "Company is decidedly *de trop* at a time like this."

"You will stay and be thanked like the proper gentleman you were raised to be," the old woman told him.

No one had spoken to Wynn like that in over six years. He had braved barren wildernesses and sailed most of the seven seas. He had made his fortune in a harsh, empty land, and another in a harsher one that was teeming with life. He owned a fleet of merchant ships and held shares in a myriad profitable ventures, with more men dependent for their livelihoods—if not their very lives—on him than lived in many English towns. He'd even found time to assist the Crown with delicate financial negotiations, which was how he dared show his face in town again. He was a man now, nearing his thirtieth year.

He had wealth.

He had power.

He sat back down on the brocaded sofa.

Just to prove that no maiden aunt was going to intimidate him, Wynn raised one dark eyebrow, then lowered it when he saw that Lady Ann was too busy feeding shaved ham to Homer to notice.

At least they were both somewhat more presentable now, he and his dog. After a long drink—water for Homer, cold lemonade, then brandy for Lord Ingall—the dog had been wiped clean, and Wynn had been taken in hand by the butler, Mallen, himself. His coat had been restored, sponged, and brushed. It would never pass muster, nor would his limp neckcloth, his scuffed boots, or his stained fawn breeches, but he did appear more the gentleman and less the chimney sweep. He was almost comfortable sitting on the gold brocade furniture.

He got to his feet when he heard footsteps approach the parlor door. He would bow, refute any hint of heroism, and be gone. At last.

The major domo was also restored to his proper butlerish mien, with no traces of tears or trembling hands as Mallen regally announced, "His lordship, Earl Duchamp."

Wynn started his bow, but the earl was having none of it. He was not going to settle for a polite nod, nor even a formal handshake, not from the man who had rescued his only daughter, the light of his life, from a fiery death. Or a smoky one. Lord Duchamp did not have all the details yet, but one thing was certain: he owed this gentleman an enormous debt, one he would happily discharge. He rushed across the carpet and enveloped Wynn in a fierce, back-slapping hug.

What happened to unemotional British stoicism while he was gone? Wynn wondered, locked in this stranger's embrace with no polite way of escaping. He could not recall his father touching anyone, his heir or his wife, much less the useless second son. The earl, though, was red-eyed from crying, but beaming now. Perhaps the volatility was a relic of Duchamp's French ancestry, for otherwise he was the pure British squire, ruddy cheeks, square jaw, thin sandy hair—and bulldog determination to pound his joy and gratitude into Wynn.

Only Lady Ann's caustic "You are embarrassing the boy, Daniel," made the earl drop his arms and step back. He wiped his eyes and blew his nose, then waved the butler forward with his tray of champagne glasses.

"A toast!" Duchamp declared, to Wynn's relief. One drink and then he could leave.

When they had each been served, a saucer on the floor for Homer, the earl held his glass high. "To you, brave lad."

"To your daughter's health," Wynn quickly appended.

"And to her future happiness," the earl said with a wink. "But we will speak more of that at a later date, eh? Torrie told me about her vow."

Now Wynn's neckcloth had wine spots on it, from where he choked on the champagne.

The earl handed him a napkin. "They've given her laudanum, so I'll hear all the tidbits in the morning, but I could not be happier, my boy."

Wynn could not be happier, either—not unless he was boiled in oil, stretched on a rack, or hung by his thumbs. *Those* were preferable fates. Before the earl could post the banns, Wynn hurried to say, "You must ignore the lady's so-called vow, my lord. I fear she was in shock. Any other woman would have been suffering paroxysms"—to which, thank goodness, Lady Torrie had not subjected him, only this ninnyhammer's notion of a wedding—"but she could not have been in her right mind."

The earl's smile faded as he sipped his champagne. "Still, never known m'girl not to know her own mind. I would have seen her shackled a hundred times over, otherwise, these three years past." He brightened, even as Wynn's hopes of avoiding an awkward situation dimmed. "It's early days yet."

Wynn carefully placed his empty glass on the tray.

"Quite. But this one grows late, sir, so you will have to excuse me." From another drink, from a daft damsel's pledge, and from the earl's embarrassment when he heard the gossip about Wynn's name. The viscount was determined to take his leave.

"Of course, of course. Not every day a fellow gets to play Sir Galahad, eh? Wearisome business, rescuing maidens, eh?"

He'd never know how wearisome. The last one had cost Wynn six years. He stepped toward the door.

"But what can I do for you in the meantime, sir?" the earl insisted, following him. "A horse? No, I am sure Mallen will already have my carriage waiting to see you home. My tailor's direction? You'll send the bill for a new coat to me, of course."

"No, truly, I need nothing." He nodded toward the earl's sister. "Lady Ann has been everything kind."

"Surely I can do something for you. My gal means everything to me, you know."

Wynn knew. He also knew how the earl's stance would change when he learned about the old scandal. "No, nothing. Seeing the lady restored to her loving family is ample recompense for what, in truth, any man would have done."

Lady Ann made an unladylike noise. "George St. Brenner did not so much as soil his gloves."

"What, that man-milliner was at the dress shop? Likely having lace sewn on his unmentionables." The earl dismissed Lord Boyce with another swallow of champagne, but returned to his resolve to reward Wynn somehow. "I know. I've never seen you at White's. I shall put your name up at my clubs."

Wynn could not let this kind man suffer the ignominy of having his protégé blackballed. "Thank you, but I doubt I will stay in London long enough." He studied his ruined boots, understanding that the earl would not wish to be so indebted to another man. "You could . . . you could give me the name of a reputable employment agency. I fear my new valet will give notice after this day's work."

He did. The third valet in a week left Wynn's employ. The first one, Nolan, was so old his hands shook, not something one could overlook while being shaved. The next, Andrews, was too short. He could barely reach to adjust Wynn's neckcloth, and there was something about the petite chap's poetical dark looks that did not feel right in a gentleman's boudoir. This last one, Herne, Wynn thought his name was, had the airs of a duke. Dog hairs sent him into a tizzy, but the afternoon's grime had him throwing his hands in the air. This was not what a gentleman's gentleman had the right to expect, he announced on his way out the door, leaving Wynn in the same sorry state as when he entered his Division Street lodgings in Kensington.

Viscount Ingall had a fine town house in fashionable Mayfair, fully staffed, he was certain, from the size of the household accounts. Any number of footmen could have served to help him dress. The butler could have shaved him. The potboy could have polished his boots. Why, his deceased brother's valet might yet be on the premises, the salaries at Ingram House were so extensive. Unfortunately, his deceased brother's widow, Marissa, was most likely also in residence. Wynn had not checked. He preferred his modest rooms away from his sister-in-law and away from the *ton*—until it came time to hiring a valet. The premiere valets refused to take up such an unfashionable address, with so few underservants. High-nosed Herne had been the last man on the nearest personnel agency's list.

"At least I got the name of a new employment service," Wynn told his man-of-all-work, who never seemed to work at all. "With the earl's recommendation, they are bound to send over a reliable, respectable man at last."

Barrogi grunted. "Your fancy neck pieces need a

snake charmer, not a caper merchant, *padrone,* they have so many ends."

Wynn held the soiled one he was unwinding from his neck. It had a beginning and an end, that he could see, but Barrogi had never mastered the knack of tying a proper cravat—on purpose, Wynn suspected. He never managed to get a shine on a pair of boots, either. A world traveler whose mostly Italian ancestry was as muddled as that of Homer the dog, Barrogi could speak thieves' cant in six languages, and knew the back alleys of at least twenty foreign cities. The short, broken-nosed man might be a fugitive from justice in all twenty, but he'd proved invaluable to Wynn the past few years, especially at gathering information.

The viscount intended to send Barrogi out again, this time to discover what he could about Lady Victoria Ann Keyes, Lord Boyce, and Madame Michaela's dressmaking shop, but not until Barrogi stopped at the Day & Day Placement Service, and not until Wynn had a bath.

"Hot water, she is not good for a man," Barrogi grumbled as he hauled the cans of water. "Softens him, like a Chinook about to be plucked."

"A salmon? Don't you mean a chicken?"

"*Nondimeno.* Same difference."

Wynn did not care. The hot water felt heavenly, especially when he added a drop of that oil the smooth-skinned little valet had left. It felt even better when he leaned back in the copper tub, a glass of brandy in one hand and a cigar in the other. He had not realized how sore his muscles were from the rescue, nor how many cuts and bruises and burns he'd accumulated without feeling them at the time. He hoped Lady Torrie was not so afflicted. It would be a crime to mar the perfection of that pale skin he'd caught sight of.

Maybe the steam was melting Wynn's brain after all, making him think warm thoughts of the earl's disturbing daughter. Hell, he already had more women in his life than he knew what to do with.

He had a former mistress who was breeding and wanted to marry him to give another man's child his name.

He had another former mistress who was outrunning the duns and wanted to marry him to pay her bills.

He had a former sister-in-law—he supposed his brother's widow was still his sister-in-law, unfortunately—who wanted him dead. Barring that, Marissa wanted him respectably married, thus restoring luster to the tarnished family name. Not surprisingly, she had an impeccable candidate for his bride already selected: her cousin.

No, the last thing Viscount Ingall needed was another woman trying to push, poke, or prod him into parson's mousetrap. No matter how pretty he imagined her to be.

Chapter Four

Barrogi returned with information and a valet, thank heaven and the earl's intercession. The gentleman's gentleman was a strapping fellow, as big as a Canadian moose, and he obviously took pride in his calling. After introducing himself, he walked around the viscount, then declared Lord Ingall a well-set-up cove who would advance his, Larsen's, reputation. The weathered complexion would fade, he allowed, and, of course, a suitable wardrobe would have to be ordered, one befitting a viscount, not a vagrant. Wynn's fumbling, out-of-practice attempt at tying his own neckcloth was instantly replaced with something Larsen termed the Triple Crown, which was certain, Wynn knew, to impress the most discerning eye. He was sorry to tell poor Larsen he'd merely be dining at a dark coffeehouse with some business associates, not Carlton House with the prince.

Larsen shrugged as if to say a pub today, a palace tomorrow, and immediately set to inspecting Wynn's meager wardrobe and rearranging his bedroom.

Wynn happily left him to it, joining Barrogi in the sitting room to hear his tidings. His right-hand man had his left hand wrapped around some of Wynn's best port, and he was lounging in the most comfortable leather armchair the room offered.

Wynn poured himself a glass of wine and raised his brow. "Odd, I thought you were an employee here, not a guest," he hinted.

"You want my news or not, *padrone*? You seemed panting like the dog to learn more about the, how they say it? The gentry mort before."

Wynn took a seat on the couch, and Homer jumped up next to him to have his ears rubbed. "That's a lady we are talking about, my friend." A seat and a sip were one thing, a gentlewoman was another.

Barrogi nodded, heeding the warning. "I had to lay out much of the *denaro* to get the details so fast. No time to befriend the servants."

Wynn nodded. "You will be repaid, as always."

"Just checking, *padrone*. Now that you are wrapped like a present and smelling sweet as roses, I wondered."

Wynn loosened his neckcloth. The Triple Crown was now a Double, more fitting for a merchants' meal. "Go on."

Barrogi's information only confirmed what Wynn already knew or suspected: Lady Victoria Ann Keyes was the belle of this London Season, and had been for the last three. She was pretty as a picture, well educated at a fancy finishing school, and wealthy in her own right from an Irish laird grandfather's bequest, to say nothing of the handsome dowry her father offered. The Duchamp earldom would fall into abeyance with her father's passing, but the lands and fortune were not entailed, so Lady Torrie, as she was called, stood to be one of the richest heiresses in the kingdom. She would bring to her marriage more money than a man could spend in a lifetime, and more than any one man deserved. Besides the blunt and the breeding, her strawberry-blond looks and her father's influence, the female could ride, sing a sweet tune, dance like a dream, and stay on the good side of all the old biddies. "A regular paradox," according to Barrogi.

"A paragon?"

"Same thing, in a woman."

The Keyes Diamond, they also called her, Barrogi

went on, especially in the men's clubs' betting books, where her name figured frequently.

"Fussy female, they say," he added, "although no one says the mo—the young lady puts on airs. Just that she has not settled on a suitor yet, but not for lack of offers."

Boyce's name was often linked to the lady's in the wagering, although his odds of winning her hand were not considered favorable. His odds of going to debtor's prison were a lot better, if the cents-per-centers did not choose more permanent ways of making good on their loans.

"Punting on River Tick, is he?"

"More like swimming with the sharks. No one thinks he is swift enough to outrace them."

"A lot of noblemen live beyond their means, hoping for a windfall or a lucky wager. Does Boyce stack the deck?"

"You mean does he cheat? If so, he has not been caught yet. Your *Elegantones* will game with *un oumo* what beats his footmen and tups his maids, but they do not hold with a Captain Sharp."

Wynn took another swallow of wine. "What about Madame Michaela?"

"The mantua-maker? Now, there is *una femmina* what bends the truth like a braided rug. A regular—how do you say?—straw damsel she was, Dora Mickles, until some rich cit set her up in trade. All the nobs go to her on account of her free-for-alls."

"She holds mills?"

Barrogi screwed up his face. "Laces and stuff."

"Ah, folderols."

"That's what I said. Smuggled goods. Dorrie, she does not give anything away for free."

"Could someone be trying to put her out of business? A competitor, perhaps, if she is so successful, or a rival smuggling gang?"

Barrogi shrugged. "Who is to say? Perhaps one of the wealthy aristos did not like her new gown, no?"

"Look into it, will you?"

Wynn decided to do some investigating of his own after supping with his business contacts. He walked Homer back the way they'd gone earlier this afternoon, to the alley by the dressmaker's shop. He poked through some of the debris and detritus left by the fire brigade, and knelt to sniff at a damp spot near the rear door. Soon the viscount's gloves were stained with an oily substance, his knees were torn on the sharp splinters, and his coat was covered in grime when he picked up the dog before harebrained Homer could step on an ember.

The fire was arson.

An invitation to call on Lady Victoria Ann Keyes waited back on Wynn's mantel.

And his new valet quit.

Torrie was not having a fine evening, either. Her head hurt from the laudanum. Her throat was raw from the smoke. And her parents were arguing.

She was alive, so would not complain too much about the aches and pains; she did protest as loudly as her poor throat would allow about her mother and father's quarrel.

"I say she cannot marry that man," Lady Duchamp was saying from the right side of Torrie's bed.

"I say she gave her word," Lord Duchamp countered from the left.

"He told you himself our girl was not in her right mind. He will not hold her to the offer."

"I knew precisely what I was saying, Mama," Torrie whispered from the depths of her pillows. Both of her parents ignored her.

The earl pounded his fist on his knee, which sounded like a hammer inside Torrie's poor aching head. "Well, she gave me her word, by George. I told her she could marry the man of her choice, and this is the chap she has chosen."

"Fate chose him," Torrie tried to say, but her words were lost as the countess uttered a phrase she would have chided her husband for using. Torrie pushed herself up on the pillows so her parents could no longer ignore her. "He saved my life, Mama," she said.

The countess took Torrie's hand. "I know, my darling, and for that I shall be eternally grateful. But not grateful enough to hand him my most precious gift." She turned back to face her husband. "I say offer him a reward, an estate, a fortune, the Irish stud."

"My Irish stud?" Lord Duchamp was taken aback for a moment, thinking of the magnificent hunters he'd acquired along with his magnificent Irish bride. Then he rallied. "You heard the girl. He saved her life."

"And he will ruin her life. Is that what you want for your daughter?"

"Now, Maggie, you cannot be sure the chap is a loose fish."

Margaret, Lady Duchamp, might not have an international espionage agent to hand, but she had something equally as effective: the servant's grapevine. She knew all about Wynn Ingram, the recently elevated Lord Ingall. "The man is an outcast. His reputation is so tarnished he will not be received in polite company."

Daniel, Lord Duchamp, brushed that aside. "With my influence and your social standing, he will be invited everywhere."

"Not when it is known that he fought a duel."

"Pish-tush," her spouse chided. "Young men have always fought duels, illegal or not. Some old hotheads do, too."

"And do any of them have to flee the country for killing their opponent?'"

"Lynbrook was a dirty dish who deserved to die. If he weren't godson to one of the king's ministers, the whole affair would have been swept under the rug. They were making an example of young Ingram, was all."

"Everyone says Ingram was the guilty party. He should have fired in the air instead of aiming to kill Lord Lynbrook."

The earl felt the need to inspect his fingernails. "Now, now, you cannot know what went on at the field of honor that day."

"I know there was no such thing as honor!" Lady Duchamp cried. "His own family disowned him for the deed. They say an acquaintance helped him flee the country and lent him a stake to live in the Colonies or some other heathen country."

"A stake which he used to make his own fortune." Lord Duchamp had his own sources of information in the servants' quarters. He was not about to give his girl to any basket-scrambler, no matter how many acts of valor the chap performed.

"We are not speaking of money, we are speaking of moral fiber. Would you let your daughter marry a here-and-therian who . . . who . . ."

Torrie's aching head was swiveling between her parents. "Who what?" she demanded.

Lady Duchamp brought her lace handkerchief to her lips. She had been feeling ill lately, and the day's events had upset her constitution even more. All she wanted was to take to her bed, but not before she made her pigheaded husband and his stubborn daughter see reason.

"Normally I would never speak of these things to you, Torrie. Ladies are raised to pretend such wickedness does not exist."

"Don't go all mealymouthed on me, Maggie," the earl said. "The gal is twenty years of age. She's been out for three years. Do you honestly expect me to believe she does not know about . . . about . . ." When it came to it, Lord Duchamp could not discuss . . . fornication with his wife and daughter.

"Do you mean birds-of-paradise and the like?" Torrie asked, rescuing both her parents. "Light skirts? Cyprians? Everyone knows men keep mistresses."

"Not all men," her father quickly clarified, noting the icy glare from his pale-faced lady.

"No decent husband," Torrie's mother added. "No honorable, loving husband would so demean his wife by keeping a . . . a paramour."

"Was that what the duel was about? Lord Ingall—or Mr. Ingram as he was then, I suppose—and Lord Lynbrook were fighting over a mistress? But the viscount was not wed then, so it would seem Lynbrook was the villain of the piece, since he was married."

Neither the earl nor the countess met her eyes.

"Oh," she said after a moment's reflection. "Ingall's mistress was Lord Lynbrook's wife?"

The earl harumphed. "Hearsay only. There was another female, a faro dealer, I think."

Torrie had to have a drink of the barley water at her side. "Ingall had two mistresses?"

"He could not have been more than three and twenty," her father blustered. "A mere lad down from university. Wild oats, don't you know, water under the bridge. There's no saying he won't make a decent husband now."

"Tigers do not change their stripes," the countess insisted. "Any woman who thinks she can reform a rake into a faithful husband is a fool, and no daughter of mine could be that featherheaded."

"Well, no gal of mine goes back on her given word. I say she marries the man."

"And I say she does not. Just how many vices must Viscount Ingall have before you consider him unfit for our child?" She counted off on her fingers: "The man is a womanizer. He is a wanderer. And he is a onetime murderer."

Chapter Five

"Ah, Maggie-o, you cannot know that. Men can change. I was not such a steady old chap in my youth."

"You never fought a duel."

"No one ever threatened my beloved."

That quieted the countess, that and Daniel's use of his old pet name for her, Lady Margaret O'Neill that she used to be, daughter of the laird.

Torrie tried to speak, but her father went on: "And I would challenge any man who dared offer you insult today, for you are still my beloved, and still the most beautiful woman in the world."

"Gammon," the lady replied, although a tender smile played about her lips. "You know I have lost my shape, and my hair is beginning to show gray."

Duchamp would have taken her to their rooms right then, to show his lady wife how perfect she still was in his eyes, and in his arms, but he recalled his daughter's presence. And his daughter's unmarried state. "Duels are not the point. Besides, Ingall could have changed. Having to make his own way in the world could do that to a lad. They say he has a cool head for business, and there are whispers of service to the Crown. That means he's a loyal Englishman, despite being tossed out. None of the other frippery fellows hanging on Torrie's skirts have done anything for the country."

"You would not permit a soldier to woo her, fearing she'd follow the drum!"

Lord Duchamp ignored that. "The viscount could be tired of his travels and wanting to set up his nursery. He's the last of his line, according to Mallen, who knows his Debrett's better than his Bible. At least we know Ingall ain't after Torrie's dowry."

"But he is not after her heart, either."

"That can come in time."

"What if it doesn't? They would have a lifetime in a wretched marriage. I wanted better for her. I wanted what we have."

The earl had to walk around the bed to take his beloved in his arms, no matter who might see. "Ah, Maggie-o, so did I. So did I. But would you not rather have her wed to a brave lad who has proved his worth, than to no one at all? Don't you want to hold your grandchildren in your arms?"

Lady Duchamp started weeping, to her husband's and daughter's consternation. "No, no," she said when they would have called for her maid, seen her laid down in Torrie's bed, or called the physician back. "I am merely weary and overwrought at the thought that we might have lost Torrie. I cannot see her lost again, this time to a libertine."

"But . . . but the man is good to his dog," Duchamp said, making one last try.

The look Lady Duchamp gave him, despite her tears and her wan complexion, could have withered an oak, much less an earl. "Men! Faugh." She stiffened her backbone, and her resolve. "Well, if you pursue this course, Daniel Keyes, and this man, you do it alone. I will not stay in town to watch my daughter make a *mesalliance,* nor will I help establish a criminal in society's ranks. I am returning to Dubron." She named the family's country seat, in Yorkshire.

"You'd travel to York, now, during the Season?" Lord Duchamp could not believe his ears.

"That is what I said. I am exhausted by the social rounds and the constant need to be somewhere every waking hour."

She had been looking sadly pulled, the earl admitted. "Then you can accept fewer invitations, attend less balls and such."

"No, I miss my roses."

"But you hate the smell of the sheep."

"I hate the stink of London worse. I shall simply grow more roses. I am adamant. I am going to the country."

"I shall go with you, Mama," Torrie finally got a chance to say, her father having sputtered to a standstill.

"No!" they both shouted, knowing she would never marry if buried in the downs, with naught but the sheep herders for company.

"But I cannot stay here without a chaperon," Torrie pointed out.

"Your aunt is companion enough, with your father's escort."

"You mean *I* have to go to those infernal routs and ridottos?" the earl yelped.

Torrie could not match his volume, but her indignation was his equal. "Aunt Ann distrusts all men!"

"Then perhaps she is the best one to advise you about this ill-conceived notion to wed a man of such ill repute. I cannot be party to the travesty of selecting a life's mate on a moment's whim. It is contrary to everything I— everything I thought we—believed about love and romance and marriage. Why, you might have thrown your suitors' cards into a hat three years ago, Torrie, and been done with making your choice long since. Your chances for happiness would have been greater."

She reached over and stroked her daughter's cheek. "You and your father will come join me for the summer. If you have settled on this course, you can be married from the Duchamp chapel, the same as your father and I were, if the roof does not collapse under the weight of such hypocrisy. Recall, you will be vowing to love, honor, and obey this chance-met churl. Decide carefully, my dear, not in the heat of the moment, not in the heat of Madame Michaela's fire."

After listening to her father rant and rage for twenty minutes, Torrie feigned fatigue. When he finally left, to complain about female perfidy to his friends at his club, Torrie tiptoed into her mother's chambers, feeling like a child again. The physician had ordered Torrie to stay in bed for at least three days, and any member of the well-meaning household staff would have reported her disobedience.

Lady Duchamp was supervising two maids in packing her trunks.

"You are really leaving us, then, Mama?"

The countess dismissed her helpers. "We will easily finish this later. After all, I will not be needing most of my finery in Yorkshire." Then she turned to Torrie. The fact that she did not immediately order her daughter back to bed was an indication of Lady Duchamp's distraction. "Yes, I really am going away. I am quite looking forward to some time for solitary walks, to read my books, and of course to work on my gardens. You know I have not been feeling quite the thing these last few weeks. A sojourn in the country is sure to lift my spirits."

"As I cannot." Waves of guilt were washing over Torrie as she realized how much of her mother's time had been wasted dragging a finicky miss to Venetian breakfasts and waltzing parties. She never had an inkling that her mother so disliked the social whirl. Why, she was making herself ill while Torrie danced through her slippers and suitors. "You and Papa were right. I . . . I should have wed years ago. Sir Eric—"

"Would have made you a dreadful husband, as handsome and sweet-natured as he was. He was too young to know his own mind. Why, he still dangles after a different miss every Season."

"Then Lord Brondale."

"Who would have gone through your dowry in a year."

"Major St. Leger?"

"Would have bored you in a week, reminiscing over his war experiences and recounting his wounds. No, you did right to refuse all of them."

"On your advice. Can you not stay and help me now, Mama? I truly need your wisdom. You do not have to accompany me anywhere you do not wish to go. Aunt Ann—" Torrie tried not to shudder at the thought of having the sharp-tongued spinster act as her duenna.

"Marrying is a decision you have to make for yourself, my darling. Just use your heart, and not just that thick head you inherited from your father."

Torrie tried to smile, but she could not help feeling that she was being abandoned. "But how will we go on without you here?"

"The same as you will when you have a household of your own to manage. This is good practice for you."

"Papa will miss you terribly."

"As I shall miss him. We have not been apart for more than a sennight since we wed over two decades ago."

"Then don't leave, Mama," Torrie pleaded, the rasp in her voice more from tears than the smoke's effects. "I need you. I do not know what to do!"

"Silly goose, you are three years older than I was when I wed your father, and I knew precisely what I was about. Your heart will give you the answers. And I have to leave town."

"You . . . have to?"

Lady Duchamp led Torrie to the chaise and drew her down, placing a blanket over her legs and pressing a cup of tea into her cold hands. "Yes. I shall tell you why if you promise not to tell your father."

Torrie's mind was working furiously. Was Lady Duchamp being blackmailed? Could she have a lover back in Yorkshire? Had she gambled away her pin money at silver loo? No, none of those, not her mother. She nodded. "I promise."

The countess smiled. "I am breeding. I was feeling so down pin, I consulted a physician and he confirmed my suspicions. Do shut your mouth, dearest. Your tea is dribbling on my blanket."

"A . . . a baby?"

"Yes, and do not be so shocked. I have not yet reached my fortieth birthday, you know. Some women produce infants well later in life. I thought my chances of providing your father with an heir were long over, to my regret, but now there is a possibility. Or at least of another baby girl for him to cuddle and coddle."

"A baby brother or sister." Torrie could not get over it. She jumped up and urged her mother to take her place on the chaise. "Of course you must rest, and naturally you would want to be home at the Hall. Papa will be in alt." Then the excitement drained from her face as her mother studied the fringe on her shawl. "You do not intend to tell him, do you?"

"Not yet. I cannot. You know how he would wrap me in cotton wool. You are doing it already. And he would insist on coming with me to Dubron."

"As well he should. We will all go, of course."

"No. That is why I shall not tell him until the summer. You and he must stay in London and find you a suitable husband."

"Oh, Mama, what is a husband to your new baby? I can always find an eligible *parti* in Yorkshire."

"What, among your father's tenant farmers? Those are fine men, I am sure, but they cannot offer you the life you are used to living. And I refuse to have you dwindle into a perpetual aunt, like Lady Ann."

Thoughts of turning into a replica of her acerbic aunt did not appeal to Torrie, either. "Then next year. I'll meet the perfect man next year."

"When I shall be less able to escort you to town. No,

you needs must wed this year, and before the *ton* discovers my condition. Think, darling, if I have a son, you will no longer be such an heiress."

"Fustian. I have Grandfather's fortune."

"But not your papa's greater wealth."

"Fine, then I will have fewer fortune hunters dangling after me."

"You will have fewer gentlemen from which to make your choice. Poorer men can make good husbands, but they would never dare approach you if they cannot keep you in style. No decent man would, at any rate."

Torrie could see the sense in her mother's reasoning. "Still, I would rather be with you!"

"Bringing your beaux along with you? Filling the house with lovesick swains who are not in your league? No, dearest. I want the peace and quiet of my gardens. I thought to hold your children in my arms next, not a babe of my own. I wish time simply to relish the notion. You and your father will do fine here for a few months. And your aunt is wise in the way of the world. She can guide you in choosing a mate."

"Aunt Ann thinks all men are philanderers or fortune hunters or fools."

"Good. That will balance your father seeing them all as prospective sons-in-law."

Chapter Six

So Torrie wrote the note to Lord Ingall, asking him to call in the morning. She wanted to thank him, she told herself and Mallen, when she asked the butler to see her message delivered that evening. Of course, she did. The man had saved her life. But she wanted to take a good look at him, too. She recalled dark hair and skin, but that may have been the soot and smoke. She recalled a hard chest and a firm, muscular grip, and that could not have been buckram wadding. She recalled feeling safe and protected—and that she could not have felt in a rake's arms.

So was Lord Ingall a hero or a hell-raiser? Was he the best man to have in a crisis, or the worst to have as a life's companion—or both? She could forgive his history for, as her father had said, the past was past, and years had separated the viscount from a hey-go-mad youth. She could tolerate his ostracism from the *haute monde,* if her father's efforts at getting a pardon from the prince did not remove the blot on Ingall's name. With the viscount's reputed wealth, he would be accepted in any other social circles, and Torrie enjoyed country life. She thought she might enjoy travel, too, if his business or sheer wanderlust took him abroad again, so that was no strike against his lordship, either. But his mistresses . . . Ah, his mistresses.

Concubines, odalisques, dockside doxies—the journeying peer must have seen them all, and known them all. Could he be content with one woman, one wife, one partner? Torrie could accept no less. What if she grew to love him? Would she have to watch him spread his affections among the *demi monde,* or among her own acquaintances, with other noblemen's wives? That would be a living hell, indeed. She had seen ladies of the *ton* pretend their husbands were not driving by in the park with painted women. She had seen those same ladies slip away from dances to meet their lovers in dark corners. She had pitied them all, and had sworn not to follow their examples.

A marriage without a deep and abiding love appeared to be her fate, but Torrie would not enter into a union without mutual trust and respect, which meant honoring one's marriage vows. Her mother was right: Torrie could not wed a womanizer.

Yet she needed to marry more than ever, and quickly. She had vowed to do so, for one thing, and her father could join Mama in Yorkshire as soon as a betrothal was announced, for another. For a third reason, if she needed one, the talk of babies had made Torrie envious of her own mother. She wanted a tiny infant of her own to hold, not a baby sibling.

She had, however, already asked Wynn Ingram, Lord Ingall, to marry her. The viscount would not hold her to the offer, Papa had said, made *in extremis* as it was. But he had saved her life. . . .

The agency the earl had recommended was very efficient. Wynn had a new valet bringing his morning chocolate. This one's name was Clemson and he came with high recommendations, and a higher salary than any of the others. His hand was steady shaving Wynn, and he had a good eye for selecting an ensemble suitable for calling on an earl's daughter. Unfortunately, and unforgivably, he threw a bottle of cologne at Homer. He swore it was an accident, that the dog's barking had made him lose his grip on the bottle, but his aim seemed too good for a bit of carelessness. The dog had a cut above his eye, and Wynn had no valet, again.

"Thunderation!" he cursed. "Now I have to tie the blasted neckcloth myself." For half his years abroad, Wynn had not worn a neck piece at all. Starch and white linen were as rare, and as useless, in the wilderness as they were in the jungle or onboard a merchant vessel. A knotted kerchief had sufficed. For the other half, he'd had someone to wrap the wretched things. He could tie a double half hitch in the dark, he could weave snowshoes out of vines and twigs, but he could fly to the moon before he tied a proper Waterfall or a *trône d'amour*. And he was calling on an earl's daughter.

"Here," he said, handing a fresh length to his so-far unhelpful assistant, "you tie it."

"Me?" Barrogi answered. "I am no *valletto*."

"Well, I can't and Homer won't. That leaves you."

Barrogi held up swollen-jointed fingers that had ended his pickpocketing profession years ago. His own neck was bare except for a dirty cord that held a gem-studded cross, the provenance of which Wynn was always reluctant to ask. "Just make a knot and slip it over your head, *padrone*, like a noose," the older man suggested now. "You look like you are going to face the hangman anyway, no?"

Maybe he'd go visit Rosie first, Wynn considered. After all, her impending motherhood was one of the reasons he had returned to England at all. He'd sent a bank draft, but he had been putting off a personal visit, guessing it would turn entirely too personal. Rosie Peters was certain to know how to tie a man's neckcloth, though, having untied so many in her illustrious career. Somehow he doubted that Rosie would be as eager to help if she knew his ultimate destination. She'd rather put a ring through his nose than a bow around his neck.

Lady Lynbrook might or might not know how to fashion a gentleman's cravat. Lord knew the baron's widow did not know how to balance a bank account. Wynn had sent Bette another check, but he knew he would have to go visit her soon, too, once he'd girded himself against her tears and tantrums, say in another six years.

Then there was always Marissa, his sister-in-law. Wynn doubted the haughty female could see a man's neckcloth, she held her own nose so high in the air. Furthermore, if he appeared at her house—his house—in his undress, she'd thrust her cousin into his arms, cry compromise, and see him wed before sunset. Most likely she had a special license just awaiting his call. He'd call on Beelzebub first.

Or the earl's daughter. Wynn had to admit Lady Torrie seemed the best of the lot, if a trifle attics-to-let. That was understandable, he told himself, after her close brush with the afterlife. She would be a perfectly behaved young miss today, he was certain, as boring as beef broth and as stiff as . . . as the blasted starched linen he was trying to wrap around his throat.

She had not seemed stiff at all in his arms yesterday, he recalled. She'd felt just right, in fact. He wondered if she was as pretty as they said, or if she had her mother's red hair. Lud, he had to go, simply to make sure she suffered no ill effects from the fire, and that there had been no other attempts on her life. No, he'd let Barrogi question her maid and the other servants about that while he did the pretty in the drawing room, damn it.

Perhaps he should tell the earl of his suspicions. Wynn remembered the man's exuberant greeting, though, and his toast, and hoped Lord Duchamp would be at his club or Parliament or anyplace but home. Wynn could put a flea in the butler's ear. Having to face Lady Duchamp, Lady Victoria, and the crowlike aunt was enough for any man.

Botheration.

He grabbed up another length of fabric, the last untried, unwrinkled one, and quickly, with firm and practiced movements, knotted it around his neck. Triple

Crown? Hell, the finished product did not even resemble a tiara.

"What do you call that?" Barrogi asked from the door.

"The beaver pelt bundler. It is sure to become all the rage." Wynn studied himself in the pier glass, then shook his head. He would have to do.

"Do not forget the flowers," Barrogi called after him as he left.

Wynn turned. "Flowers?"

"*Sí*, females like that kind of thing."

The last thing Wynn wanted was for Lady Victoria to see him as a suitor, but he had not been raised in a pigsty, and knew he ought to bring a token to show his regard. "What kind of flowers?"

Barrogi shrugged his shoulders. "Something that smells pretty. You know, in case your dog . . ."

"The dog is not—"

Homer was at his feet, wagging his tail. "Right," Wynn told him. "This is all your fault. You can carry the blasted bouquet."

The butler was not on duty when Wynn arrived at Duchamp House. A bewigged footman was. He took one look at the soaking dog—there had been ducks to chase in the Serpentine—and the spattered gentleman, and tried to shut the door in their faces. "The family is not receiving."

All of Grosvenor Square could have heard Wynn's sigh of relief. He handed the servant the bouquet of violets the flower girl in the park assured him were every girl's favorite, and drew out his card.

"Oh, you are *that* gentleman. They've been awaiting you, my lord. This way, sir. May I take your, ah . . ."

Wynn did not wear a hat or carry a walking stick. His ruined gloves had been left in the park.

". . . your dog?"

Homer was already inside, though, already trotting toward the parlor where he'd been treated like visiting royalty yesterday. Wynn took a deep breath and followed.

The butler looked up from where he had been arranging the tea things and nodded his approval when the footman showed Wynn in. Neither the earl nor his countess were present, but the room still seemed full, to Wynn. Lady Ann's lips curved up at the corners, and she set aside her needlework to offer him her fingers to salute, but Lady Victoria beamed.

She was as beautiful as rumor had said. Dressed now in pink silk with a matching ribbon threaded through her red-gold hair, she was a confection. She was perfection. There really had been a diamond under yesterday's ashes. Her smile was as brilliant as any gem—as it slid past Wynn to rest on his dog.

"Homer!" she called, inviting the dog, damp as he was, to join her on the sofa, closer to the plate of biscuits.

Lady Ann cleared her throat.

"And Lord Ingall."

The earl's daughter finally looked up at him. Wynn could see that her eyes were the blue of tropical waters and her lips— No. He studied the hand she offered him, instead. Gracefully formed, it was, with long fingers and skin that felt like— No. He kissed the air the polite two inches above her hand and dropped it, like a burning— No.

He sat and accepted a cup of tea. And a macaroon. And a small slice of poppy seed cake. Lady Ann went back to her needlework.

Wynn inquired about Lady Victoria's health.

She hoped his was as good.

He asked about her parents.

She asked about Homer's.

He thanked her for another macaroon.

She thanked him for the violets, her favorites.

He commented on the weather.

She wondered about storms, on his recent crossing to England.

If the talk got any smaller, Homer would be leading the conversation. The events of the day before, and the marriage proposal, lay between them like a sleeping dragon they feared to awaken. The dragon was not going to fly away, though, not without burning a hole through Lady Duchamp's Aubusson carpet.

"I think Homer would enjoy seeing our gardens," Lady Victoria finally suggested, nodding toward the French doors leading to a rear terrace. "And I could do with some fresh air. Will you accompany me, Lord Ingall?"

He looked over at Lady Ann, hoping she would throw a lifeline to a drowning man, but she said, "No, I am content right here. You two go along. I can watch from inside."

She could watch him sink, Wynn despaired.

Chapter Seven

Catching up her paisley shawl against the spring chill, Torrie led her guest out the glass doors and down the terraced steps to the walled-in garden. The season was too young for many early blooms, but the greening shrubbery made a pleasing venue for a quiet talk. The dog immediately ran off to investigate the hidden corners of the garden, and the viscount looked as if he wished he could disappear, too. Well, this was not going to be an easy conversation for her, either, Torrie thought.

She pointed to a nearby bench and his lordship nodded. He did not take her arm as most gentlemen would, but he was a palpable presence at her side. If there was one thing she remembered most about the fire's aftermath, it was the sure, solid comfort of this man. She'd felt safe with him, as though nothing more could harm her, not while he was near. She still felt protected, despite all that she had learned about her rescuer. Whatever else he might be, she would wager her fortune that Wynn Ingram, Lord Ingall, would never knowingly harm a woman, or raise his hand against anyone weaker than him.

He did not look like a rake. In fact the viscount looked like an interesting, attractive gentleman, somewhat out of the ordinary mold. While they were having that torturous tea with Aunt Ann, Torrie had taken stock of this man she might marry. His clothing was made of expensive fabrics, if not tailored to the height of current styles. The cut and colors were conservative, except for his neckcloth, which was tied in a knot she could not recognize. Torrie liked that, a man who did not follow fashion's dictates but set his own mode. He had dark hair that was less combed in the Windswept than actually tousled by the day's slight breeze. She liked that, too, both the lack of oily pomatum and the lack of artifice. His skin was indeed as dark as she recalled, from the sun and not the smoke, then. He looked like he could be at home aboard ship or in tropical climes—or riding a Thoroughbred cross country. He would have been an outright Adonis, she decided, if his nose were less prominent. According to her father, that nose ran in the Ingram family. The previous viscount, an undersecretary in some cabinet post, had a regular beak, according to Papa, one that matched the eagle on their family crest. He'd died a year ago, but Torrie did not recall meeting him at all the come-out balls, musicales, and theater parties she had attended. She would have remembered the current viscount. This Lord Ingall, Torrie knew, would turn every woman's head.

He did not have the eyes of a rake. She had expected a hardened libertine, a ruthless trader, a man drawn to violence to have dark eyes, cold, glittering ones, or pale, reptilian orbs. Lord Ingall's eyes were a lovely green, almost the color of the moss that grew on the nearby dolphin fountain, but a more vibrant shade, with tiny orange and gold specks dancing in them.

He did not act like a rake. In fact, he kept his distance, instead of trying to touch her with any excuse, or brush against her. He sat as far away from her on the stone bench as possible without falling off the end. Torrie enjoyed not being crowded, for once. She had air to breathe, air pleasantly scented with the faintest trace of lemon and spices from his cologne.

He did not talk like a rake, with innuendo and false flattery. No Spanish coin for this wealthy gentleman.

None of which, of course, proved he was not a rake. Torrie sighed. After three Seasons of being pursued by every wellborn, would-be seducer, she thought she could recognize one of their ilk. Lord Ingall did not match any of her notions, so how was she to know? She sighed again.

"Are you certain you are well enough to be out walking?" he immediately asked. "Your lungs might still be suffering ill effects."

"No, I am fine, truly. My foot shows the only lasting damage, and that is minor." She raised her hem slightly, so he could see the bandage on her ankle. She did not mean to be flirtatious, but was curious as to his reaction.

He looked dismayed, not dissolute. "Dash it all, I am sorry."

She let her skirt drop to its proper length. "Why should you be sorry? You did not cause that shelf to collapse."

"No, but I should have been there faster, or been more gentle moving the fallen debris."

"Nonsense. You could as easily have been a moment later—a moment too late. The entire building could have collapsed around me. You were there, right on time, though, the answer to my prayers. That is why I proposed we marry."

There. She'd said it. Out in the open.

The viscount jumped to his feet and started pacing. "Fustian. You were out of your mind. In shock. Delirious. It would be better for both of us to put that unfortunate conversation out of our minds. I assure you, I will gladly forget marriage was ever mentioned."

Torrie touched the chain that held the diamond-studded key around her neck. "I cannot forget."

The viscount turned to face her, his lips thinned in anger. "I do not know what kind of game you are playing, Lady Victoria, but I refuse to take part."

"It is no game. It is my life, my future. I made a vow, you see."

"To whom? If this is between you and the Almighty, I swear I have not been in His good graces for years. I doubt He even recalls my existence."

Torrie was not about to get into a discussion of faith and fallen sparrows. "To the Fates, then. Or to myself. I promised that if I was saved, I would wed, to make my parents happy and to fulfill my destiny."

"Marriage might be your destiny, madam, but it is not mine. If you choose to be subject to such superstitious tripe, then wed with my blessings, for what they are worth. I will even send you a silver candlestick. I am certain any number of gentlemen will be lining the path to your door for the opportunity to light that candle— Uh, to fulfill your pledge. Lord Boyce comes to mind."

"He does not come up to my standards, however." Torrie pulled the key charm out of her bodice and held it in her hand. "He does not . . . That is . . ." How to explain to a stern-faced stranger that Lord Boyce did not stir her heart? "I cannot see spending my life with a man who . . ."

"Wears a puce waistcoat?" Lord Ingall offered with scorn in his voice, as if poor taste were her only reason for rejecting so ardent a suitor. Torrie noted that his own waistcoat was a light gray, with narrow dark blue stripes that matched his Bath superfine coat.

"No," she said. "I have other reasons for believing that Lord Boyce is not the man for me." He was foolish and boring and narrow-minded, to list a few, but mostly she did not love him.

"Well, I am not the man for you, either."

She held firm to her beliefs, and to the talisman at her neck. "I asked for a favor, and you arrived."

"You were not making a bargain with your maker, then, you were cutting a deal with the devil." He held his arms out. "Look what such a foolish barter brought you. You should have negotiated for better terms, if you were wagering your soul."

"I was hoping to live," she said softly. "And I see a

gentleman, I think, one who is better than some. Many men would have leaped at the thought of wedding my father's wealth."

"You see a man worse than most, barely entitled to be called a gentleman. Forget your smoke-born fancies. They were phantasms, only. Why, I am not even accepted in your world."

"You would be, with my father's help."

"I make my own way." He turned his back on her then, calling the dog to heel so they could leave. "And you know nothing about me."

"I know they say you killed a man in a duel."

"*They* say a great many things."

Torrie noted that he had not outright denied the charge. She had no way of finding what she needed to know except by asking, and nothing to lose now except a primrose plant the dog kept digging at. "Did you murder Lord Lynbrook?"

"I shot him. He died. Does that answer your question?"

Not exactly. Torrie persisted. Although the viscount still faced away, he had not left yet. "No one is certain if the duel was fought over his wife or his mistress."

"Why not both? The *ton* certainly considered me capable of it."

"If you were the guilty party, they say, you should have deloped."

"What, and let that dastard shoot me? That is the most buffle-headed thing you have said yet, my girl. He would have shot me through the heart, yes, and left me lying in the field for the crows to pick. Even my fate was better than that."

"But you were the one blamed."

"Lynbrook and his brother had the ear of the king's ministers, who decided to make an example to other wild youths. As a second son, I was considered expendable in the name of justice. Since my own family believed the worst, they were pleased to have me shipped off, rather than be held to trial where I might have defended myself. The gossip would die down faster that way," he added in a bitter tone.

"So your actions *were* defensible."

He did not answer, but Torrie could see the way his shoulders straightened and his head rose. Here was a proud man, not ashamed of his deeds. Either he was totally without scruples, or he believed he was right. More thankful than ever that Aunt Ann had stayed inside, Torrie dared to ask: "Tell me, my lord, do you approve of a married man keeping a mistress?"

He spun around. "Good grief, have times changed so much since I have been gone that gentlewomen speak of such matters in public?"

Torrie could feel the blush rising in her cheeks, but she answered, "We are not in public, sir."

"Where is that devil-spawned dog?" Ingall muttered, calling out to Homer again. The dog ran over, and jumped in Lady Victoria's lap, leaving muddy footprints on the pink silk. "Dash it, I am sorry. Let me—"

She clutched the dog closer, bent on holding it hostage until she had her answers. "You were giving me your opinions, my lord?"

He was giving her a set-down and they both knew it, but the viscount answered, more or less: "Do I approve of a married man having a light skirt in his keeping? I do not believe a man has the right to keep his wife pregnant every year of their marriage, until she is old and worn years before her time. I do not think a woman ought to marry a man for his fortune and then not give him his money's worth in bed. I do not approve of fathers selling their daughters into unhappy marriages for their own gains. I see no reason for land and titles and wealth to be the foundations for many marriages, instead of mutual affection and respect. I could go on to speak of brothels where children are held in bondage, of fatherless infants left to starve in the gutters, of hollow-eyed beggar women dying of the pox. You see, ma'am,

I do not approve of many things your society accepts. If, however, you are asking me if I would be a faithful husband, my opinion does not matter, for I never intend to put it to the test."

"You do not intend to marry?"

"At last, she sees reason." He spoke to the dog.

"That is not reasonable. What about your title? The succession?"

He laughed. "My father never cared whether I lived or died. Neither did his heir, my brother Roger. My closest living relation is dear Roger's widow, who never ceases to mourn the fact that I am alive and he is not. The succession can go hang, as I almost did."

"But you survived."

He nodded.

"And prospered."

He nodded again.

"They say you made a fortune in the fur trade."

"Which shall all go to worthy charities when I am gone. My man of affairs has the list."

"And another fortune in spices or tea. Papa was not sure which."

"Both. Fortunately, or unfortunately for the poor souls involved, there are a great many worthy causes."

"Then you do not need my father's money."

"I need nothing from any man. Or any woman." He glared at Homer before turning on his heel. "Or any dog."

Chapter Eight

Torrie let the dog go. He was not hers to keep.

She let Lord Ingall go. He was not hers, either.

She let her dream go, the dream that danced through her veins, humming about true love and the perfect match and lovers who were destined to meet against all odds.

What she could not let go of, however, was her gratitude. The viscount might not be the answer to her prayers, he might not even be a very comfortable companion, but he had saved her life. "Wait!"

He turned at the terrace steps, one dark eyebrow raised as if in expectation of her next impertinent question or outlandish proposition. Underlings would have thought twice about their next words, when they saw that disdainful gesture. As usual, Torrie forged ahead.

"I merely want to say thank you again. Your selfless actions might seem insignificant to you, but, I assure you, they meant everything to me. Other men would have stood aside and let the hired firefighters rescue me, and who knows if they would have been in time. Another man might have left me to my own devices outside the building, shivering in my shift. Why, you could have handed me over to Lord Boyce for the drive home, to listen to his importunings while I was in distress. Instead you preserved my life and my dignity, and never ceased until I was home safe. I know there is nothing I could possibly offer to show my appreciation, nor my father,

his. I can think of no reward that you would accept,
but . . . but I would like to be your friend."

The female wanted to be friends now? Wynn shook
his head. What did he need with a spoiled darling of
society for a bosom bow? Very well, he conceded, Lady
Victoria seemed a decent sort, not flying into a rage
when she did not get her way, nor turning into a watering pot. And he would like to see her smile again, for
him this time, instead of his dog. But he had never had
a female for a friend. Rosie did not count; he had paid
for her affection. Lady Lynbrook was not a true friend,
although he had known her for ages. Wynn was more
like a footman she called to fix things. They both always
wanted something from him. Lady Victoria seemed to
want nothing but what she asked: his friendship. But what
would he and Lady Victoria talk about, the latest gossip,
the newest styles in bonnets, her next proposal? Or perhaps the widgeon wanted to tag along with him to mills
or race meets, like Homer.

On the other hand, he had employees and dependents,
but no real friends in England. His old school chums
and boyhood acquaintances had turned their backs on
him quickly enough when he was disgraced. The only
one who did not, the friend who helped him start a new
life in the new world, had since died a hero's death in
Spain. And despite himself, he did feel a tie to Lady
Victoria. Having carried her to safety, he could not turn
his back on the young woman now, especially when she
might still be in danger. As a friend, he would be more
able to keep an eye on her, to look out for her. Wynn
felt a lot better at the thought—but it was impossible.

"I fear we will not have the opportunity to become
more familiar," he said with true regret. "I doubt we
will be traveling in the same circles."

"I never supposed you would attend Almack's, if that
is what you were worried about. I cannot even convince
Papa to accompany me there. I think you will find most

other doors soon open to you, however. Mine will always be."

He bowed slightly, touched by her kindness and sincerity. "I thank you. And while I am about it, I must apologize for my churlish behavior. Instead of cutting up at you before, I should have said that I was deeply honored by your offer, and thanked you. That is the proper way to refuse a suitor, is it not? Never having received a proposal of marriage before, nor given one, I am not quite certain of the correct form."

She smiled as he'd intended. "That's precisely what they taught us at Lady Castangle's Academy. And I must apologize also. I should never have made so precipitous an offer in the first place. You were right. It must have been the smoke clouding my judgment. I will forgive you if you will forgive me."

"Done."

"Friends?" She held out her hand.

This time he took it and shook it, as he would with a gentleman. "Friends." Her smile was so enchanting, so genuinely pleased with their bargain that Wynn instantly forgot they were supposed to be comrades. He brought her hand to his mouth and kissed it.

Lord Duchamp was disappointed, but not surprised. He was waiting for Wynn in his library, a large room that yet seemed homey, with its worn leather chairs and smells of old books and pipe smoke. He was hoping for a formal petition for his daughter's hand. What he got was a view of the viscount's back heading down the hall toward the front door and freedom.

"I told Maggie that bird would not fly," the earl muttered when he sent his butler after the man, to invite him in for a drink. "But she had to go and make a big to-do over a minor matter. That's women for you." He nodded a greeting when Wynn entered the library, then directed him to take a seat while he reached for a decanter of Cognac. The dog found a comfortable spot on the bearskin rug in front of the fireplace.

"I see you have not got that matter of a valet straightened out yet," Lord Duchamp said while he poured, gesturing with his glass toward Wynn's neckcloth. "I'll have a word with the Day brothers at that employment agency of theirs. Have you looking fine as five pence in no time."

Wynn sipped his wine and said thank you, trying not to rip off the offending article or plant the earl a facer. What else could he do but be polite, having just refused to become the man's son-in-law?

The refusal was on Lord Duchamp's mind, too, and he did not beat around the bush. "I don't suppose if I double the dowry you'd change your mind?"

There was not enough blunt in the Bank of England to change Wynn's mind. He did admire Lord Duchamp's plain speaking as much as he admired the library's floor-to-ceiling bookcases, though, and the wide windows letting in the day's light. He could be content with a room such as this, if he had it to himself, Wynn thought. He shook his head. "No. I have more than enough brass for my needs."

"It couldn't be that my girl ain't pretty enough, could it?"

"Lud, no. Lady Victoria is a true incomparable."

"Almost as pretty as her mother, I always thought, but I might be a shade prejudiced. Smart, too, and well educated, my gal. We sent her to Lady Castangle's Academy to get rid of her Yorkshire accent. Nothing wrong with it that I could see, but my Maggie said it had to go, so off went Torrie to school. Lud, how I missed her. You'd never guess how much that Castangle woman charged, either."

"No, I am sure I could have no idea." Except it was bound to be dear, making the headstrong chit conform to someone else's standards.

"Another female caught your fancy, then? I suppose

you must have seen any number of pretty gels on your travels, prettier even than Torrie. I wouldn't be surprised if they all took to dropping their handkerchiefs to catch your eye, what with your fortune. Not to say you aren't a bang-up chap, with a title and all now, but the women do look at a man's bank account first, eh?"

The deuced neckcloth was strangling Wynn. He might as well be a blasted bearskin himself, pegged out to dry, the way the earl had his personal life laid out in public. He gulped a sip of Cognac past the knot at his throat. "No, no. I have not, ah, fixed my interest with any woman."

"You ain't one of those . . . ? That is, you don't prefer . . . ?"

"Good heavens, no! I assure you that, were I looking to get leg-shackled—that is, married—I would search no further than your lovely daughter. I am simply not in the, ah, marriage market, I believe they call it."

"Ah, well, you cannot uncork the wine before it's ready, eh?" The earl set his glass down and sighed in resignation. "So what are your plans, if you don't mind an old man's prying, if you don't aim to settle down? More travels?"

Wynn did not care if he never saw another crowded cabin on another storm-tossed ship. Neither could he see burying himself in the country on the family estate in Hertfordshire. He'd stopped there on his arrival at Bristol, to make sure his steward's reports were accurate and the place was in good heart, and to try to recall any fond memories. There were few enough, as he was sent off to school at an early age, and never encouraged to know the lands that would one day belong to his older brother, the heir. The steward, Bimm, was a weathered turnip of a man, seeming to have roots in the earth himself, and was delighted when Wynn gave him *carte-blanche* for improvements and modern equipment. It appeared that the previous title holders, Wynn's father and brother, never cared to waste their blunt on their own lands or tenants, which added to their sins. As soon as the old man had started in about which hogs to purchase, Wynn had left.

He supposed, if he gave up traveling and chose not to rusticate, he could set up an office here in town and make himself another fortune. For what? The thought had been on his mind for months, ever since he considered returning to England. He was a young man, not yet thirty. What the devil was he going to do with the rest of his life?

"I have not decided what I will do," he told the earl. "I have some business and personal matters to take care of first, then I will consider my options."

"The reason I ask is, we could use some good men in the party. The government is going to hell in a handcart, what with the war and the riots and the Regency bills. Your brother—"

"I am not my brother."

"Of course not. Couldn't be. He's dead. But if you mean you ain't ambitious like he was, there's plenty to be done without putting yourself forward. I have some friends coming to dine this Thursday. Mayhaps you'd—"

"No, thank you. I—"

The earl held up one hand, flashing his heavy signet ring, reminding Wynn that he had not gone to the vault at Ingram House to claim his yet. His sister-in-law most likely guarded it like a dragon its golden horde.

"Hear me out," Duchamp said. "Can't blame you for thinking they'll be a parcel of old bores at the table. Most will be. But think about the invitation a minute. Even if you don't want to go into government, these are men making laws that will affect your business. At the least, they are deep-pocketed peers, interested in making investments, like your shipping lines. They'll hang on your every word. And if you are thinking that some of the high-sticklers will cut you, think again. Not at my table, they won't. No one would dare insult one of my guests, and especially not the man who saved my little girl. It'll be a good introduction back into society for you."

"And if I said I did not care about reentering the ranks of the upper ten thousand, what then, sir?"

"Then you'd be a fool. Not that I'd blame you. Happier in Yorkshire myself, raising a pint with my tenants. But a man cannot always choose where he takes his mutton, and it'll always taste better among friends. Someday you might decide to go courting. Hell, someday you might want to present your daughter at Court, or bring your boy to Tattersall's. Don't shut the doors in their faces now, when you can open them with a few hands of whist and a bottle of port. You don't have to walk through those hallowed portals yourself, mind, just make sure they are open to you and yours."

This was the second time today someone had spoken of doors opening, when so many had been closed to him for so long. The viscount had not made his fortunes without listening to sound advice when it was offered, and Duchamp did seem to have Wynn's best interests in mind. Besides, Wynn thought he just might wish to see the inside of White's Club again, or speak to some person of authority at the War Office without having to steer through the subalterns. "Thank you, my lord. If you are certain I shall not discommode your guests, I gladly accept your kind invitation to dine."

"Good, good. We can use some livelier company at these deuced dull affairs, and I know Torrie will be happy to have someone near her own age."

"Torrie? That is, Lady Victoria will be there?"

"Of course. Hostessing for me, don't you know, since my wife decamped, uh, decided to leave early for our country pile. Redecorating, don't you know. Torrie will do fine. You can help her and my sister entertain some of the old witches—uh, the wives of my associates."

"Wives? You never said there would be women at the dinner."

Wine, women, and Whigs, oh, hell.

Chapter Nine

W ynn's new valet was caught stealing. Barrogi had him pinned to the wall with a long, narrow blade at his neck, an emerald stickpin having fallen from his pocket onto the floor. The viscount had not even had time to memorize the miscreant's name, Randall or something, much less if he were any good at putting a shine on a pair of boots. The man had tears in his eyes, knowing what he'd done was a hanging offense. Barrogi wanted to haul him off to the authorities—except that he did not want to show his own distinctively battered face at Bow Street. Wynn was all for shipping the thief to Botany Bay—but only if he could go along.

What the devil was he doing, breaking bread with a bunch of political boors, blowhards, and bunglers . . . and their biddy wives? No matter what Duchamp might think, the females would pull their skirts aside when he walked past, the gentlemen would refuse to partner him at cards. Lady Torrie's—Lady Victoria's, that is—party would be ruined. What a way to start a friendship, destroying her credibility as a hostess. He'd warned both her and her father how it would be, but to no avail. They were clinging to their attempts to restore his respectability as hard as a chased cat clung to a high branch of a tree. Their positions were all precarious.

"So are you going to take the gallow's bait to the wrong house or not, *padrone*?" Barrogi wanted to know.

"The roundhouse? Dammit, I do not have time for

that." Wynn had two days to order a new wardrobe, eradicate curse words from his vocabulary, and hire himself a new valet. He supposed he also ought to get around to calling on Rosie and Lady Lynbrook and solving their dilemmas, so his troublesome past could stay in the past where it belonged. The stack of their letters, forwarded by his man of affairs, was threatening to overflow the mantel. While he was at it, he should see about dislodging his sister-in-law from Ingram House. If by some remote chance he was to become acceptable again, he would need a proper gentleman's residence with an exemplary address. His present remote hidey-hole would never do, nor would a staff that consisted of a half-gypsy bandit holding a knife on a varlet valet. Oh, and he had to catch an arsonist.

"So you want I should cut his hand off, the way they do in those heathen countries?" Barrogi offered.

The valet whimpered.

"What, and ruin the carpet? These are rented rooms, remember. Besides, that seems a rather drastic punishment, doesn't it, considering Randolph never got out the door with the jewelry. Perhaps it just fell into his pocket while he was tidying up."

The man nodded vigorously, or as vigorously as he could with the point of a very sharp blade pressed to his throat. "That's it, your lordship. I was just cleaning up."

Barrogi was disgusted. "You mean to let him go, *padrone*?"

"I mean to have a few words with Mr. Day and his brother. They really have to do better than they have been doing. When I am through, I expect Rudolph here will find himself without references or another chance of employment. Of course then he might take up the life of crime on a more permanent basis, which is not doing any kind of justice to the rest of the population. No, I think it will have to be the ships."

"Not New Zealand, your lordship," the valet pleaded. "Not that!"

Wynn studied the slim but wiry valet. "No, you'd be wasted there, if you survived the journey. I can always use good men on my merchant vessels, though. What say you to a berth on a clipper ship, with pay? Of course, if the captain finds you stealing, he'll toss you overboard. It's either that or take your chances with His Majesty's justice. Decide quickly, Rupert, for I am in a hurry. I have to learn to be a gentleman before Thursday."

Someone else was having trouble with his neckcloth, but that may have been because a hired ruffian had him by the collar. Worse, it was his own hired ruffian. Worst of all, the thug expected to be paid.

"What d'ye mean, I didn't do the job? I set the fire just like we planned."

"You set three fires, you dolt!" the gentleman shouted. "You burned half the place down instead of creating a disturbance."

The henchman stopped throttling his employer to scratch his head. The gentleman stepped back, out of range of the long, thin, apelike arms, and downwind of the apelike odor. He straightened his clothes and shuddered to think of what creatures might come crawling out of that stiff, strawlike mop of hair. Tall and reed-thin, dressed in rusty black, the felon-for-hire was called the Hay Man, or Scarecrow, and he was all the gentleman could afford. If he'd been able to part with one of his snuffboxes, he might have hired a more competent co-conspirator, but then how could he match his every ensemble?

Scarecrow spit on the floor, barely missing the gentleman's sequin-studded shoe buckles. "The first faggot didn't catch on anything. The second jest made a lot of smoke. It were the third what did the trick."

"The trick was not to kill the girl, by Jupiter! What good would she be to either of us dead?"

"What good is she now, is what I wants to know. You

was supposed to have a roll of soft, soon as you had 'er rolled up."

"The cents-per-centers would have made me an advance against expectations, if I could have announced a betrothal. Instead your blundering had her running right into another man's arms, blister it!"

"So you want I should disappear the flash cove what drug the gentry mort out of the ken?"

"Huh? Oh, no, Ingall is not worth killing. He's no danger to my plans. Not accepted in polite circles, don't you know."

The only polite circle Scarecrow knew was at Ma° Johnstone's nunnery, where he could never afford the girls. He never would, if he didn't get paid. He growled.

"No, Ingall is no threat. The earl will toss him a purse, then toss him out on his ear. He's not fit to touch the lady's hem, and her loving father will be well aware of that fact. I'll make sure of it."

"So what then?"

"So we need a better plan, that is all. I *have* to have Victoria Keyes, the key to her father's fortune! I'll have to think about it."

And Scarecrow could think about the whores at Sukey Johnstone's. They were neither one nearer their goals. Scarecrow spit on the floor again, giving his opinion of his employer's mental agility. "Meanwhile I'll be thinking how much to charge when I go sell your cold body to the surgeons' school, iffen I don't get paid."

Torrie's mother had been right, as usual: one should not simply plight one's troth to the first chance-met stranger on the street. A woman had to be discerning where she bestowed her hand, for she would also be giving the gentleman the rights to her fortune, her body, and perhaps her heart, for all time. She had to know his character, his moral fiber, his attitude toward children if he was to father her unborn babies. After all, she would be married for life—the same life Wynn Ingram had granted her.

On further reflection, Torrie had decided not to give up on Viscount Ingall as a marriage prospect. No matter what he thought of her vow to wed, she was still committed to finding a husband, if not just any husband, before much longer. She had promised herself, and promised her father, too. Both of them wanted to be done with this courtship business before much longer, so they could be reunited with Lady Duchamp. The viscount was still Torrie's favorite contender for her hand, despite the fact that Lord Ingall did not consider himself in the running.

Her father liked him, which was an excellent indicator of his mettle—or Papa's desperation to return to Yorkshire.

Aunt Ann did not dislike him, which was an even bigger factor in the viscount's favor.

And Torrie thought she could come to like him very well indeed.

Lord Ingall was different from all the other men she knew, and not just because he was well traveled. He was a successful businessman, for one thing. He actually did something with himself besides gambling and drinking, the apparent occupations of most *tonnish* gentlemen. Further, the viscount was not interested in making a name for himself in the upper echelons of society, he was not interested in Torrie's money, and he was barely interested in Torrie herself. No, she thought, he was not like any other man of her acquaintance.

She hoped she was not shallow enough to be piqued by his lack of attraction to her, nor challenged to chase the unattainable. Those would be hen-witted reasons for settling on any gentleman, and bound for disappointment. No, she really believed her rescuer might make a good husband, if he could be convinced that he wanted a wife.

Foolish fancy or what he called superstition aside, Torrie supposed she was naturally predisposed toward the man who had saved her. Ingall *had* been the one, not Boyce or the other preening pea-geese who wrote paeans to her lips. What was a poem in her honor compared to being hauled from a burning building? Torrie was not going to be taking a quatrain to bed, was she? She wanted a strong, brave . . . virile husband.

Torrie felt herself blushing to be having such warm thoughts about Lord Ingall, a man she hardly knew. She was a properly brought-up female, after all, who should not keep recalling how her fingers had quivered for hours after he had kissed them.

She was also the girl who had stayed up at nights at Lady Castangle's Academy, giggling with the other students over the Italian art books. How many females could look at Lord Ingall's broad shoulders and narrow waist, his ruffled curls and his firm jaw, and not feel warm thoughts?

Aunt Ann, for one.

"I am not saying he is not handsome, nor a decent man." Torrie's aunt paused to rethread her needle—before she figuratively burst Torrie's bubble with it. "I am saying he will not make you a comfortable husband, if you can bring him up to scratch, as your father so vulgarly puts it. You will not wrap one like that around your finger."

"But why would I want a weak-willed husband, Aunt Ann, one I could keep under the cat's paw? I would not wish to wed an overbearing tyrant, of course, nor a man who believes women have nothing between their ears but feathers and fluff. But why not wed a man who would treat me as an equal, as his friend and lover?"

"Hmph. You have been borrowing those novels from the lending library again, haven't you? Borrowing trouble, that's what."

Torrie thought that inviting the viscount to her father's dinner party was an excellent idea. While furthering their friendship, she could learn more about his character, and he could take his rightful place in society.

No matte what else, both Torrie and her father were determined to reward the viscount by restoring his standing among his peers.

Once he saw that he was welcome in London, perhaps he would stay in England. If he stayed, he might grow fonder of his heritage, and thus change his mind about the succession. He might simply tire of his bachelor state. Who could tell? He might even discover that there were actually a few successful marriages in the world.

Everything had to be perfect for the dinner Thursday, so Torrie spent hours with the seating charts, then made sure via the servants that the guests learned of his heroism. She had to teach Lord Ingall that not everyone was close-minded and judgmental, or holding the past against him. She also had to show what a good hostess she could be, so she spent hours with the cook and the butler, wasting the time of both of those proficient souls. Of course she wanted to be in her best looks, so hours more were needed to dissect her wardrobe, inspect her complexion, and select the proper hairstyle. Her maid, Ruthie Cobb, who was still feeling poorly, was ready to hand in her notice.

Torrie had time for one additional chore. She added Lord Cooperstone to her list, and the old curmudgeon's beautiful, young, and—according to the latest gossip—discontented wife.

The dinner would be educational for all of them.

Chapter Ten

Somehow Wynn never found time to call on his erstwhile Erinyes, the three female Furies who had
helped ruin his life six years ago. Thanks to them, he
had given up his carefree wastrel boyhood to become . . .
a man of fortune and power and values. Perhaps he did
owe them something, at that, some courtesy beyond paying their pressing bills. He'd see about it. After the dinner. For certain.

He was too busy now, getting Rufus on a ship and
ordering new formal wear, and paying six times the price
to have it ready in time. He did not wish to shame Lady
Victoria more than his presence had to. Nor, he admitted to himself, did he want her to look on him as a
barbarian.

He met with some of the newly wealthy merchant
class who were all too eager to have him to *their* houses.
No matter the condition of his wardrobe or his reputation, they always happened to have a daughter or a
niece. He refused their invitations to dine or take tea,
deciding he really ought to have an office of his own for
these meetings.

And he met with Mr. Day, the elder. The younger
fled by the back door when he heard Wynn's angry voice
in the front office. Wynn was assured that the agency
would not fail him again, most definitely not, for they
were honored by his patronage, to say nothing of Lord
Duchamp's. They had just the man for him, a Spaniard

who had served a highly placed *grandee,* before his support of the French troops ended his life, not so grandly. He would be at Wynn's front door on Thursday, the day of the dinner.

When he arrived for an interview, Viera swore, in Spanish, that he would be the finest valet the *señor* ever employed. Then he repeated it in English. *Sí,* he liked *los perros.* No, he did not mind living in El Kensington.

"What about neckcloths?" Wynn asked, wanting to make doubly sure this fellow would serve his needs.

Viera assured him, in Spanish and in English, that he tied the *corbata* most *magnifica.* He curled his lip at those *idiotas* who needed nine lengths of cloth to attain one creditable knot. Why, he, Viera swore on his sainted mother's grave, could tie the complicated Waterfall in less than four attempts.

"No, no, I do not want anything so intricate."

In that case, Viera would only need three linens. Any more and he would consider himself a failure, *un malogro.* In fact, he swore, if he could not please *Señor* Ingall in *tres* tries, he would resign. *Sin dinero.* Without pay.

Wynn hired him, and Viera moved in the next day, the day of the Duchamp dinner. Wynn's bath was the right temperature, his hair was trimmed to the right length. His new clothes were brushed and ironed to an inch of their nap, from his chapeau, which he would carry, not wear, to his midnight-blue coat, to his white satin knee breeches, to his clocked white stockings. His new leather evening pumps only pinched a little, but *Dios,* how they shone.

Wynn held his breath as Viera took the top white cloth from the pile of three. Barrogi held his breath. Homer held his breath. Viera smiled briefly, then became intent on his task. He stood in front of the viscount. He moved to the back. To the front. To the back, winding as he went, almost faster than the eye could follow.

Then he stood back and clapped his hands. *"Perfecto,* no?"

Well, no.

Barrogi was snickering behind his hand. Wynn looked at himself in the mirror, at the huge bow that flowed halfway down his chest. He looked like a blasted birthday present. He cursed, but in Hindi, to save the eager Spaniard's feelings.

Viera understood enough to know Wynn did not like his creation. "To low, *sí*? No matter. I fix."

He pulled the offending bow off and reached for the second cloth. This one he worked on for twice as long, deliberating over every crease and fold. Finally he told Wynn to lower his chin. Wynn could not. He tried to turn to look in the mirror, but he could not see downward and so tripped over Homer, who yelped. So did Wynn when he got a glimpse of himself with his nose facing nearly skyward and his chin jutting out of a snowy mountain.

"Too high, *señor*?"

Definitely too high. Wynn was supposed to be eating dinner at the Duchamps', not inspecting the chandelier. He took a sip of the wine Barrogi held out to him, to settle his nerves.

No one spoke as Viera reached for the third and last length of fabric. Viera studied the cloth, studied Wynn, shook his head a few times, then nodded. *"Sí.* The *Elegante*." And he got to work.

It was superb. Not too showy, not too dull. *"Perfecto, amigo,"* Wynn told the grinning valet. "Pour yourself a glass of wine. You deserve it."

Viera did, and clicked his glass to Wynn's in celebration. The Spaniard was a bit too relieved, though, a bit too exuberant. A drop of Madeira leaped out of his glass . . . onto the neckcloth, which was now not so elegant at all.

Viera sobbed as he walked out the door. Wynn would

have cried, too, but not in front of Barrogi, who was trying to be helpful.

"Tell them you thought it was a masquerade," he said. "You can wear one of those banyan things, *padrone*. Call it a toga or a mongoose or something."

"A burnoose?"

Barrogi nodded, then said, "A man who cannot wipe his own chin ought to grow a beard, no?" which was equally as helpful.

Wynn sighed. It would have to be the beaver-pelt knot again.

Most of the guests were already assembled when Wynn arrived at Duchamp House for dinner. His reception was mixed. Lady Victoria seemed relieved that he had shown up at all, which bothered him, that she could doubt his word—or his bravery.

Of the other women, one's welcome was a trifle icy. Most were tepid. One was torrid. Wynn had seen the look on Lord Cooperstone's young baroness's beautiful face before, on the lieutenant governor's daughter, on one of the officers' wives, on an Indian brave's squaw, and on an Indian potentate's concubine. In any country, in any language, that look meant one thing: trouble. He vowed to steer clear of the old peer's young bride, easy to do since he was busy peering at Lady Victoria.

Lady Torrie, as everyone seemed to call her, was even more elegant in evening dress, more magnificent, more perfect—they all sounded better in Spanish—than when he had seen her last. Perhaps this was because there was less of her pink silk gown, and more of the earl's daughter to be seen and admired. Now he could barely take his eyes off what he had been too much of a gentleman—and too busy saving her—to notice on the day of the fire. Soft, creamy mounds rose above the lace trim, like twin pillows a man could dream on, like snowy mountains he could climb, like . . . like whitecapped waves that an unwary sailor could drown in.

No wonder half the unwed gentlemen in London wanted to marry her. The other half must be blind, already betrothed, or, like Wynn, confirmed bachelors.

How the deuce was he supposed to make conversation about the current breast-seller, Lord Duchamp's ivory chest set, or the bustery weather?

He forced his gaze back to Lady Cooperstone, but his attention would not stay fixed there, even though the lady's neckline plunged lower, her russet silk gown was sheerer, and her sultry smile was more inviting. She could have been naked for all he cared. In half an instant Wynn was glancing back at Lady Torrie and the diamond key she wore, where his eyes should not go.

He was rescued from an almost worse social gaffe than killing Lord Lynbrook by the earl himself, who pulled Wynn away. He wanted to introduce Torrie's hero to some of his political cronies. Since Lady Torrie was such a favorite with the older gentlemen who had known her since birth, her savior was warmly welcomed in their midst. The notion that he, and his overflowing coffers, might join their political party was a further inducement to their hearty handshakes. After adding enough tributes to his supposed bravery to bring a blush to Wynn's sun-tanned cheeks, one of the silver-haired lords raised his quizzing glass to the viscount's neckcloth.

"Setting a new fashion already, I see, eh, Ingall? I vow all the young jackanapes in town will be trying to ape your style within the sennight. What do you call that knot anyway?"

What did he call it? The Desperation? The Last Hope? "I, ah, call it the Bundler," Wynn said.

"Named after that quaint Colonial custom, I suppose. Clever, lad, clever, how you have the ends close, but separated from each other by a pearl for virtue."

Sometimes Wynn was so clever he amazed himself, like at dinner. He managed to get through the dinner without staring at his hostess's *décolletage*. So what if she was at the far end of the long table and he was in the middle, with a large epergne in the way? He conducted himself commendably, he considered, chatting first with Lady Bernard, who had known his mother, on his left, then with Sir Spencer's wife, whose brother was serving in India, on his right. He could not have recalled what he ate, but he did remember the various charities he had promised to support with his contributions. Both ladies were well pleased with him, and followed Lady Torrie and her aunt from the room praising him to the skies, telling all of the other women what a generous man he was. They could never guess how much more he would have donated if they'd offered to move the blasted epergne.

With his hostess gone, Wynn could pay closer attention to the gentlemen. He would have, anyway, if they did anything but belch and brag of their latest gaming wins, their latest conquests. He supposed the talk of government and finances came later, when they were even more in their cups. Thunderation, he thought, this life was not for him, even though he was welcomed back into it. One of the men invited Wynn to attend the next race meeting with him, one asked him to stop by for a night of cards, and a handful wished to put his name up for their clubs. He was no more interested in those activities than he was in joining Lord Cooperstone and his bride at a house party at their cottage in Richmond.

He did not gamble for high stakes. He had worked too hard, for too long, to make his fortune to toss it away on the turn of a card or the speed of a horse. He'd rather give more of it to an orphanage than to an ivory-tuner anyday.

He did not drink to excess. A man who lived by his wits could not afford to dull them with spirits.

He did not consort with married women. Bette, Lady Lynbrook, had been lesson enough.

As for joining the clubs, male companionship might be pleasant if they did anything but gossip, as these port-drinking patriarchs were currently doing. Wynn had too long been the subject of the *on dits* to enjoy hearing them now. At least no mention was made of the duel.

After the gentlemen rejoined the ladies, a few of the former disappeared to Lord Duchamp's library. Perhaps, Wynn thought, they were finally discussing affairs of state, instead of *affaires*. Or the older gents might be taking naps. The others were getting up tables for cards, and Wynn could see that Lady Cooperstone had him in her sights, so he quickly offered to partner Lady Ann. With his head for figures, he was a skillful player, which pleased Lady Ann. They were winning easily, until Lady Torrie came to lean over her aunt's shoulder to watch the play.

Lady Ann threw her cards down in disgust when they lost the next three hands, and the others at the table began to speak of taking their leaves. Wynn almost started to relax. A few more minutes and he could go home, without having made a fool of himself. Then disaster struck.

A tiny old lady in a puce turban rapped his fingers with her lorgnette. Her name was Mrs. Reese, he recalled, and she was old enough to have known his *mother's* mother. He supposed she wanted to put forth her pet endowment, so he was ready to add another charity to the list he would give his man of affairs in the morning. But no. The old bat was throwing a ball next week. He was invited. His mind went numb, balking at every lying excuse he could think of, for refusing.

"Well?" she squawked, and he barely had time to move his hand before she could strike him again.

"I cannot. That is, I will be busy with . . ."

Then Lady Torrie walked to his side and stopped him short with a smile. Actually, it was more a gloating grin, Wynn thought, because she had been right. He was indeed being accepted back into the fold—where he had no desire to be.

"Oh, I thought you would wish to attend," Lady Torrie said now, "especially since Mrs. Reese's party is a subscription ball. All of the monies go to establish a school for London's poorer children. I have been hearing how you wish to better their lives."

The only thing Wynn was wishing was that he'd left the interfering female in the burning building.

"And Papa is busy that night, my friend," she went on, driving her point home, "so I was hoping you would escort my aunt and me."

Friend? She called herself his friend?

Chapter Eleven

What a fine gentleman he was! What an excellent husband he would be! Torrie was delighted, and not just with the outcome of her dinner party. She dismissed her maid Ruthie as soon as her gown and stays were loosened, so she could ruminate on the glorious success of her evening without the abigail's worrisome, weary sighs to ruin her happiness. She had told the ailing Ruthie not to wait up, that one of the maids could help her undress, but Ruthie had insisted. Torrie insisted that her dresser see a physician soon, if she was not feeling more the thing. Now she was glad to be alone to go over the evening's high points as she brushed out her hair, without a maid's chatter.

She had done him proud, her father had said, and Aunt Ann had declared the dinner party a tolerable entertainment.

Tolerable? It was thrilling!

Lord Ingall was no drunkard, thank goodness. Torrie had taken care to note how few times his wineglass needed refilling, and how he was not red-faced, loose-tongued, nor fumble-footed when the gentlemen rejoined the ladies in the drawing room. Torrie hated a man who stank of spirits, or one who turned into a buffoon or turned belligerent.

The viscount was not a gambler, either, despite what rumor said about his earlier days. All the way to bed, Aunt Ann had complained bitterly about his poor card sense. With his lack of concentration, Ingall would have lost his fortune ages ago if he indulged in deep play. Instead he was wealthy enough to pay Aunt Ann's losses as well as his own, thank goodness. Otherwise, Torrie would be hearing about his buffle-headed bids over her breakfast chocolate.

Best of all, Lord Ingall was not a rake. Torrie smiled happily as she braided her hair for the night. He had never looked twice at Lady Cooperstone and her abundant, available charms. Well, he may have looked, for no red-blooded man could ignore the blatant display, but his eyes had not lingered, she was certain.

Altogether, Wynn Ingram was a perfect guest, eating everything put in front of him, conversing pleasantly with his dinner partners, not getting into political arguments with some of the more dogmatic diplomats of her father's circle. One of the guests mentioned to her father on the way out that the new Viscount Ingall could go far in the Foreign Office.

And he was generous to a fault. His man of business was certain to know that at least one of the charities he had promised to support was no more than a fund to pay the lady's expensive nephew's expenses. Mallen, the butler, reported that he was generous to the servants, too, handing gold coins to whichever footman took his hat or had a hackney waiting. No one else could see this largesse, so the viscount's openhandedness was not just to impress the polite world.

Torrie doubted Lord Ingall did much simply to impress. Judging from his garb, he was not one to care for putting on a show. Not that he needed to puff himself off, she mentally approved, with intense colors and immense cravats. No, he outdid every other gentleman in the room in his understated style, to say nothing of the width of his shoulders or the muscularity of his thighs in the form-fitting knee breeches.

Oh, my, yes. He would make a fine husband! Her father doubted the man would step into parson's mousetrap so easily, for hadn't he been cautious about joining the party, and hadn't he referred all the requests for charitable donations to his man of business? No, the viscount was not going to be led where he did not wish to follow, Lord Duchamp had warned.

Her aunt warned that the gudgeon was so absent-minded, he might have forgotten he had a wife in India. Besides, Aunt Ann grumbled, the viscount might have been on his best behavior this evening, hiding his beastly side under a cloak of good manners.

Torrie did not think so. Of course, she acknowledged, she had only scant information for making her judgment: one death-defying rescue, one dinner party. She firmly believed he was a genuinely good man, though. She was almost ready to wager her fortune and her life on it, which was how she viewed marriage these days. The viscount, she was well aware, viewed the institution of holy matrimony somewhat differently.

Torrie might be closer to learning the gentleman's character, but she was no closer to winning his affections. Beyond one brief, heartwarming smile of welcome, he had done little beyond scowl at her all night. At her *décolletage*, to be more exact. She hoped he had not grown puritanical in his travels, for that would be a shame. As her father said, a dram of devilry kept a man from dullness. Perhaps he simply disapproved of an unwed woman wearing diamonds, although the key she wore was not ostentatious.

His scowl had turned to a furious glare later in the night, when Torrie pushed him to accept Mrs. Reese's invitation. Perhaps she had been too forward, Torrie worried, but it was all for his own good. Once he was seen to be acknowledged by such a high stickler, she told herself, Lord Ingall would be accepted everywhere. Besides, he might even enjoy himself. With the music and the dancing and the superlative food the wealthy Mrs. Reese always provided, he might see what fun the Season could be.

Torrie twirled around on her way to her lace-hung bed. A girl ought to dance once with the man she was thinking of marrying, shouldn't she? What if he did nothing but step on her feet and complain, like Papa? Torrie did not think she could be content with a man who did not dance, or who was so clumsy at it that she would be forced to sit out half her own betrothal ball. For a man above average height, Lord Ingall moved gracefully, befitting his athletic build. He would be a superb dancer, unless his years abroad kept him from knowing the latest steps. Perhaps she could suggest a practice session—but no, that would be too forward even for her.

The image of her skirts swirling around his legs in the waltz was an appealing one, so appealing that Torrie drew the rest of the portrait in her mind's eye as she climbed into bed and pulled the covers up to her chin. They would dance and sway, and he would hold her a bit closer than usually permitted, claiming he did not know the current social strictures. She would not complain. Then he would waltz her toward the windows for a breath of cooler air. The dream was so vivid, Torrie had to toss one of her blankets onto the floor.

He'd ask if she wished to step out onto the balcony. No, not even Torrie's imagination could picture Viscount Ingall inviting a young, unmarried female out among the shadows. She would have to ask him, then, claiming she felt overheated.

Another blanket got thrown off the bed.

He would have to go outside with her, gentleman that he was. And somehow Torrie would be in his arms. Usually she was adept at avoiding unwanted embraces, but this time she would instigate one if she had to. Just as a girl needed to know if she and her prospective husband fit well together in the dance, she had to know if she liked her would-be husband's kisses, too.

The third blanket got flung.

Torrie thought she might like Wynn's kisses very much, if she did not take a chill before then.

One week. That's what it would take to settle his business, attend the blasted ball, and leave town. Wynn did not know where he was going to go or what he was going to do when he got there, but he was leaving. He would go to Mrs. Reese's affair because it was for a good cause and because he had given his word, but that was all. London was no place for him. Next thing he knew, he would be waltzing, by George! He could see the signs already, a stack of invitations from people he did not know, or people who did not want to know him six years ago. Now they thought he was some kind of hero, a celebrity to make much of. They wanted to show him off at their parties like a trained circus horse, a pig that could count, a rake turned rich man. That same brush that had tarred him as a blackguard acted as a whitewash when dipped in gold. The *beau monde* chose to forget they'd labeled him a murderer without giving him a hearing.

Wynn chose to remember.

He knew precisely whom to thank for his sudden notoriety: Lady Victoria Ann Keyes, the same siren whose smile kept him awake all night. He knew what she intended, too, his avowed friend.

She intended to repay him for the paltry favor he had done.

She intended to make him acceptable in her circles.

She intended to make him marriageable, may the devil take her and her laughing blue eyes.

Wynn had no desire to be an eligible *parti*, by Jupiter, because he had no desire to get hitched. Lud, he did have desire, but it was not for the *ton* to take him to *its* bosom! If his new colleague wished to be kind to him, she would wear one of those scarf things in her neckline. That way he would not have to toss and turn in his bed all night, thinking thoroughly un-friend-like thoughts, of her, in his bed, all night. Bah.

"What has you in such a pelter, *padrone*? You aren't still cooking over that valet business, are you?"

"Cooking?"

Barrogi shook his head and set his tray down. "No, I went to the bakery." He helped himself to a sweet roll.

"Stewing. You mean stewing. And no, I am not annoyed about the fact that I cannot find a man to maintain my wardrobe, shine my shoes, and see that I am properly turned out. Why should I be irritated, when I have offered a king's ransom in pay for what should be a simple job of work?"

"I am glad you are not upset, because those Day brothers closed up shop for a holiday the sign read. But me, I think they were hiding in the back room in case I came there."

Wynn shrugged and bit into a roll, after tossing a piece to Homer. "There must be other placement agencies. Hell, there are unemployed soldiers begging on the streets. Surely one of them knows how to polish a pair of boots."

Barrogi was horrified. "You would take a beggar off the streets?"

"I took you in, didn't I? And Homer. Besides, I have nearly a week to find a suitable man. I do not need to be dressed to the nines for the calls I have to make."

"What, you will visit the earl's daughter in eights?"

"It's a figure of— Never mind. I am not going to visit Lady Torrie. It's the other three women I have to see before I can leave town."

Barrogi reached for the stacks of letters on the mantel.

One batch was written on inexpensive paper in an awkward hand, splotched with ink and sealed with blobs of cheap red wax. Wynn could smell the scented notes from across the room. Those had come from Rosie Peters, the bird-of-paradise who was breeding.

The second pile of letters consisted of finer quality

paper, but the florid, curlicued script was smeared, as if by tears. The notes were sealed with pink wax and embossed with a rose. A hint of those flowers wafted from the letters of Bette Field, Lady Lynbrook, the dowager baroness who was below hatches.

The third collection had black borders and precise black lettering. No frivolous perfume, no smudges or stains would dare encroach on the finest vellum or distract from the messages contained therein, sealed in black wax with the Ingall emblem. Deuce take it, Wynn's sister-in-law had usurped his signet!

"I thought *un perfetto signore* was supposed to call on his hostess the day after," Barrogi said as he handed over the cursed correspondence.

Damn if Wynn wasn't being lectured on manners now by a world-class scoundrel. Even the dog was looking up at him accusingly. No, Homer only wanted more of the roll. Wynn tossed the whole thing to the floor in disgust. Everyone was trying to make him into something he was not, the perfect London beau. Well, he would not do it.

"No, I am not calling on that managing female. Next thing I'd know, she'd have me traipsing after her through the park. You can go in my stead, though, delivering a bouquet. That ought to satisfy the conventions. She likes violets." Wynn brushed the crumbs from his hands. "Oh, and while you are there, why don't you hang about the place, out of sight but where you can see who comes and goes. To keep an eye on the lady, you know, just in case."

Barrogi smiled, showing the gap where a tooth had been. He knew. Violets? *Per Dio,* he would bring roses.

Wynn, meanwhile, had to decide which troublesome wench to call on first. He decided to flip a coin. Heads, he'd visit Rosie; tails, Lady Lynbrook. If the coin stood on its edge, he'd go see his sister-in-law.

Chapter Twelve

Rosie won, because her dilemma seemed most pressing. Pressing against the front of her gown, at any rate. The once-pretty gaming hall faro dealer, merry as a grig and up to every rig and row, was up to her seventh month, and looked like hell. Her skin was sallow, her brown hair was dull, and her eyes were swollen from crying. Her ankles, propped on a footstool, were simply swollen.

"What is wrong, my dear?" Wynn asked when she held a limp hand out to him. "Are you unwell? I know I told you to consult an accoucheur and send me the bill. Did you? Perhaps you should consult another. I thought women in your condition were supposed to be glowing."

She glowered at him. "You try carrying this weight around and see how you glow. Besides, I've been stuck in these two dreary rooms for weeks now."

Wynn would be blue-deviled himself if he had to look at the same cabbage-rose wallpaper and the same chintz upholstery every day, even if he were not worrying about birthing a bastard. "Why don't you go out for some fresh air, then?"

"Because if I do go out for a stroll, the neighbors all pull their brats to the other side of the street or snicker behind their hands. No one comes by except the day maid and the delivery boys, and they look at me as if I were a whore."

Wynn refrained from the obvious comment. There was

a fine line, it seemed, between courtesan and Covent Garden ware. Rosie knew the demarcations. Her neighbors, apparently, made no such distinction. Well, he'd be damned if he'd let anyone point their fingers at Rosie. "Come, my dear. Get your bonnet. It is a lovely day, and we can speak together in the park as easily as here. We can take a hackney there, away from your bothersome neighbors, and walk my dog a bit before it gets crowded with the fashionables. That will put the roses back in your cheeks, my girl. And after, we can go have an ice at Gunter's."

"But it is not yet noon."

"So what? I have not had a raspberry ice in decades, it seems. I used to dream about them when I was in India."

"I prefer lemon."

Rosie was already placing a cherry-trimmed straw hat on her head and tying a crisp pink bow under her chin—with admirable speed and style, Wynn noted, and without even looking in a mirror. His own knotted kerchief was already wilted.

He took her arm and said, "Good, that will leave more of the raspberry for me and Homer."

Wynn could see the curtains twitching as he led Rosie down the steps to his waiting hackney. He turned and waved. Rosie giggled, more like the gay young charmer he remembered. Perhaps he could scrape through this interview without an emotional maelstrom after all.

When they reached the park, he adjusted his stride to her slower, more ponderous gait, and put his arm around her when the path was uneven. Impatient with their dawdling when there were so many new scents, Homer ran off on his own. Few pedestrians were out so early: an elderly gentleman feeding the squirrels, which Homer chased off, a few nursemaids with their charges, whose ball Homer stole. Wynn hurried Rosie along.

Some equestrians were exercising their horses along the carriage paths, dull work, Wynn thought, compared to riding hell for leather across open country. He missed that, not having a good ride since coming to London. The viscount idly wondered how a breeding farm would fare at his estate in Hertfordshire, or if he would enjoy setting up an Irish stud, like Lord Duchamp's.

Rosie, meanwhile, tilted her face up to the sun. "You were right, lovey. This does feel heavenly."

"Would you like me to find you a place in the country, then? A little cottage away from prying neighbors?"

"Lands, no. What would I do there? Who would I talk to? For sure there would be no work for a skilled professional such as myself."

Again, he held his tongue concerning her various professions. "I had not meant for you to work. I would purchase the cottage, of course, if none are empty at any of my holdings. And pay its upkeep, naturally. Without asking anything in return," he hurriedly added, lest she think he was making her a business proposition.

"Oh, no, you have been more than generous already." She patted her protuberant belly. "With no good cause."

"Well, if you do not wish me to support you, perhaps you would like me to look into finding a home for the infant, so you can go back to, ah, dealing. I am certain one of my tenants would take in the babe if I—"

"Give up my babe?" Rosie's voice was so shrill one of the nursemaids hurried her charges away from the nearby duck pond. Homer jumped in to finish the bread crumbs. "Never! I could of done what some of the other girls do, but it's my baby!"

"Yes, yes. Of course it is, and no one is going to take it away." Wynn tried to sound soothing, instead of near panic. Lud, you'd think he stood between a mother bear and her cub the way Rosie was screeching. "But what else can I do to help, then?"

"You know what I want, Wynn. Although I suppose I should be calling you Ingall now, or my lord."

He brushed that pomposity aside along with Homer, who wanted to wipe his wet whiskers on Wynn's biscuit-colored pantaloons. The dog took off after the squirrels again. "Wynn is fine. Go on."

"Didn't you read my letters?"

"Of course, I did," he lied, having read only the first two or three. "Your letters were one of the reasons I came back to England. To be of assistance. Tell me how again, now that we are face-to-face."

"All I want is a name for my baby."

Alan? Albert? Alexander? Wynn's mind was racing, knowing full well he was on the wrong course. Hell, he was not playing the same sport!

Rosie was going on, unaware of his unease: "I want my baby to have a better life than I have, and for that he or she needs another name than mine. I can work again as soon as I get my figure back after the lying-in, and support us all, including the wet nurse. But no matter how hard I work, I can't never buy my child respect. He'll be shamed his whole life, without a father's name, and shamed of me, his ma."

"What about the father? Won't he . . . ?" Wynn was too polite to ask if Rosie even knew who the father was. He'd vowed never to duel again, but that would not prevent him from beating the man to a pulp, leaving just enough of him to stand in front of a curate.

"Gone on his honeymoon, the dastard."

"I, ah, see." He'd still flatten the dirty dish. He saw some ladies walking up ahead, so steered Rosie down a different path.

"And I thought you would marry me, instead."

"But no one will believe I am the child's father. I was not even in the country at the right time."

"That's no matter, if you don't claim otherwise. I checked with a barrister. Since you've got no close kin to contest it, no one can say my baby isn't yours."

Wynn knew how the squirrels must feel. "But I, um, never led you to believe that I . . ."

She slowly lowered herself to a nearby bench. "No,

you never gave out false hopes, not like some I could
mention, God rot his soul. But you never did get wed,
for all these years. I would of read about it when you
came into the title. So I figured you had no mind to
settle down. And I don't intend to ask you to change
your ways, neither. I don't mean you to be a proper
husband, just for the parish register. It's not your money
I am after, and don't you go thinking that it is, not for
a minute. I know you'd lend me the ready either way.
You can go off on your travels and never see the babe
if you don't want, as long as you leave him or her your
name behind on the marriage lines."

But his name was not just Wynn Ingram anymore. He
was now Wynn Ingram, Viscount Ingall. If he and Rosie
wed, and the child was a son, the boy could claim to be
Wynn's heir. That might be a good joke to play on his
dead father and brother, but Wynn was alive and he was
not laughing.

Aside from the succession, the notion of standing as
father to another man's by-blow did not sit well with
Wynn. Supporting orphanages was one thing, calling a
stranger's offspring "son" was quite another, especially
as it would be his first son. Perhaps his only. Wynn
started pacing in front of Rosie's bench. "What, by all
that's holy and half that isn't, makes you think that I
would marry you and name your child as my own?"

"Well, we did have some good times."

They were not *that* good! Wynn was wearing a path
from the bench to the base of a nearby tree. There and
back, there and back. At least the squirrels got to run
up a tree. "Those times were few, and far in the past."

"Yes, but you were always good to me. You've been
right generous whenever I've asked, even before you
had so much yourself."

"That was my pleasure, for the pleasure we shared,
not a promise to support you and your progeny
forever!"

Rosie adjusted her bonnet to a better angle. "I know

that. But you did cost me Lynbrook, you know. I haven't had a gentleman with such deep pockets since. I figure you owe me."

"I owe you?" Wynn stopped himself from squawking like one of the ducks Homer was back to chasing. Ducks, squirrels, what was the difference when he was the quarry? "How can you figure that? Lynbrook was so cruel to you, you could not wait to leave his protection."

"But he was rich."

"He was married."

"And his wife had not conceived in five years of marriage. I wouldn't be in this fix now if you hadn't gone and killed him."

"Devil take it, I thought you knew—"

"Aye, I should of known, all right." Rosie began to sniffle, her chin to tremble, her brown eyes to fill up.

Oh, hell. Wynn sat beside her and patted her hand. "You could not have been certain." He was speaking about the duel.

Rosie was not. "I should of known you'd never marry me, not a fine swell like you, a viscount and all. I was good enough for a toss and a tumble back when you was a green lad, new on the town, but now I'm just used goods. No one is going to marry the likes of me," she bawled.

Dash it, now Wynn was feeling guilty for another crime he had not committed. "Don't cry, Rosie," he begged, too late. "I never looked on you that way. Why, you are a fine girl, and I am sure you'll be a good mother. It's just that, well, were I to wed you, I could never take a wife of my choosing. And lately—"

Rosie clapped her hands in delight, her tears forgotten. "You mean you've found a lady to love? That's all right, then. I would never want to stand in the way of your happiness."

"No, I—"

"Haven't asked her yet and mum's the word." Now she patted his hand. "I understand. And who am I going to say anything to, anyhow?" She started to get to her feet, with his assistance, for the walk back to the park's entrance. But then her face and her legs both crumpled. "Oh, Wynn," she cried. "You were my last hope. What's to become of me and my babe now?"

He caught her and held her against him, thinking while she sobbed. He thought of those tattered veterans on the street corners. If one could be a valet, one could be a husband. Then he thought of the valet he'd shipped off. He could have made him marry poor Rosie, but Rudy had left too soon. Hell, he could pay some down-at-heels gambler's debts and get him out of Fleet prison—and in front of a vicar. But then Rosie and her babe would be the property of some ne'er-do-well, some brute who could steal her nest egg, beat her, sell her son to the chimney sweeps, her daughter to white slavers.

Dash it, he had not challenged Lynbrook to that duel just to have Rosie abused by another mawworm.

"I'll think of something, my dear. I swear it, and you know I never go back on my word."

Rosie wrapped her arms more tightly around him and whimpered onto his shirtfront. "I always knew you was a right 'un."

He tried to reach around Rosie's bulk for his handkerchief to offer her. He looked back up—into blue eyes wide with shock, right behind Rosie. Homer was barking a welcome. Some distance away his own man, Barrogi, was shaking his head. The rest of the world seemed to have come to a standstill, including Wynn's brain.

He could never pretend Lady Victoria Ann Keyes had not seen them.

He could never explain why his arms were around an enceinte ladybird.

He sure as Hades could not introduce them.

Wynn would not get the chance, anyway, for Lady Torrie spun on her heel, took the arm of her gray-clad maid, and hurried down a different path.

"You see?" Rosie wailed, loudly enough to be heard by the retreating women, and anyone else in the park that morning. "Decent women are always going to turn their backs on the likes of us."

"Us?"

Chapter Thirteen

Wynn wondered what Rosie meant by "us." The frail sisterhood? Herself and her babe? Fallen women and their keepers?

Perhaps it was all for the best. Now Lady Torrie would be convinced that he was no fit consort for her, which was fine. He had no desire to be her friend, not when she was proved to be just another well-bred woman ready to believe the worst of a man. Of course, he admitted, having an armful of weeping Rosie would have been hard enough to explain under the best of conditions. He might have tried, gone traipsing after Torrie in the park as he'd vowed never to do, but he had promised Rosie an ice. He was not going to go back on his word, by George. He was a man of honor, no matter what the *ton* thought, no matter what Lady Victoria Ann Keyes thought.

Then he thought again. Where was the lady's father? A footman or a groom? She and her maid seemed to be alone in the park, which would have been fine later in the day when the paths were full, or if someone had not set the dressmaker's shop on fire with her inside. Dammit, did the earl not care for his daughter's welfare that he left her unprotected, or was he so trusting of his fellow man that he ignored Wynn's hints about arson? Thunderation, Wynn would have to warn her.

He called Barrogi over and introduced him to Rosie. "You take Miss Peters to Gunter's and buy her an ice," he ordered, handing over a handful of coins. Then he added a few more, recalling Rosie's condition. "Buy her two. And whatever you want. Then see her home in a hackney, and make sure she is comfortable, all right?"

When Barrogi nodded, Wynn told Rosie that he would come see her soon. "And try not to worry in the meantime, which cannot be good for the baby, for I will come up with some solution to the dilemma. We still have two months. Oh, and Barrogi, make sure you treat the lady like fine china."

Barrogi bowed to Rosie and offered his arm. "Me, I will treat the *signora* as if she were fine Roma."

"We should not have run off like that, without waiting for an explanation. Perhaps the woman was his cousin." Torrie did not know anyone in London whose cousin wore such outlandish bonnets with such bright pink ribbons. For that matter, no respectable woman, cousin or otherwise, would be out in public in such a state of incipient motherhood. "Perhaps the lady was his cousin from the country."

"Cousin, hah." Ruthie was panting to keep up with her mistress. These morning constitutionals were never the maid's favorites, but this mad rush had exhausted her. "And she is no more a lady than she is Lord Ingall's cousin. Her name is Rose Peters, and she is the light skirt he fought the duel over."

Now Torrie gasped. "How do you know that?"

"Everyone knows Rosie. Her picture was hanging in the print shops all the time, when she was in looks. She's a dealer at McGillicuddy's Gaming Parlor, and they say she made a fortune for him. She's one of the pretty women who get men to drink more than they ought, you see, so they gamble more than they can afford. Rose Peters used to be the prettiest, and the most in demand when she was not at the faro tables. She was in Lord George Post's keeping last. The one who just married Miss Goodwin."

Torrie felt sorry for Miss Goodwin. Lord George had little hair, less chin—and a mistress. Then she felt sorry for herself and her crumbling air castles. Lord Ingall was back, and back to his old ways. The babe might not be his, but the woman appeared to be.

At least one person in the park that morning was having a good time. Lord Boyce was congratulating himself on his foresight in having the Scarecrow watch Lady Torrie's house to monitor her movements. He was more proud that he looked so complete to a shade so early in the day. Why, even the nursemaids smiled in approval of the picture he made in his yellow trousers and curly-brimmed beaver hat and tasseled Hessians.

Usually Lord Boyce was still abed at this time of the morning, but today he had arisen soon after dawn, it seemed. He had sacrificed his sleep so that he might spend an hour or so at his toilette and still get to the park on schedule. Certes, it was not every day a fellow became affianced to an heiress, and Boyce wished to look the part. The hours were worth it, if he had to say so himself, for the ensemble that ensued.

Today he would be betrothed to the earl's daughter, by hook or by crook, by fair means or foul, by noontime, by Jupiter.

He followed the path Scarecrow said she took most clement mornings, she and her maid. He passed a low-bred pair who were leaving the park, thank goodness. Females in that condition ought not be seen by delicate gentlewomen. Then he passed a young pageboy in a wig who was shouting at an ill-dressed lout whose back was toward Boyce. The bigger, older man's dog, it seemed, had raised its leg on the boy's satchel—which contained a change of clothes for his mistress, who had spent the night with her lover. Boyce shuddered. No wonder the quality did not patronize the park before midday. Lady Torrie would not, once they were wed. Boyce would insist on that.

Swinging his walking stick in what he considered a jaunty manner as he strode down the path, he looked up, pretending to admire the birds in the newly leafed trees. Lord Boyce would not know a pigeon from a partridge, and would have thrown his stick at the noisy creatures to stop their infernal racket, except his cane might have become scratched. Besides, there was Lady Torrie up ahead, speaking with her maid.

He walked closer, then stopped short. "Oh, my, what a surprise! Well met, my lady. I did not think to find any of my acquaintance in the park this early. I would never have guessed that you shared my interest in this, ah, refreshing time of day."

"Good morning, Lord Boyce, and yes, I like to come to the park before it is crowded, to have a few moments alone with my thoughts before the day's rush begins."

The hint was so broad it could have hit a barn door. But not Lord Boyce. "I feel exactly the same! The, ah, empty spaces are so conducive to contemplation, aren't they? And the air"—he sniffed delicately, inhaling the aromas of coal smoke, stagnant water, and horse droppings—"is so, ah, refreshing, do you not agree?"

"Yes, quite. Now, if you will forgive me—"

"Oh, think nothing of it, my lady. Perhaps we should continue our strolls together, to share our admiration of Nature's bounty."

"Thank you, but my maid and I are fully refreshed, as you say. We were about to leave the park." But not by the way they had come, with its stale, sordid scenery.

"What, and miss this glorious sunshine?" Boyce prayed his hat shielded his face enough so his nose did not turn an unattractive pink. He raised his quizzing glass to inspect Lady Torrie's skin and noticed the foolish chit was developing freckles, of all abominations. He would certainly put an end to these hoydenish morning walks. He replaced the glass in his pocket and held out his arm in invitation. "Surely you can walk a bit farther?"

"Do go on, ma'am," Ruthie urged. She was still out of breath but, worse, the pace Lady Torrie set had roiled the maid's uncertain digestion again. If she could pause a minute, maybe the spell would pass. "I'd be that grateful to rest right here on this bench, where I can keep sight of you and his lordship."

Torrie saw that her maid was indeed looking sadly pulled again. She'd thought Ruthie fully recovered from her malady, or she would have taken one of the footmen for escort this morning. Torrie vowed to send for the physician herself as soon as they reached Duchamp House, which she intended to do as quickly as possible. "No, you will be better off at home. We will walk back slowly and hire a carriage at the park gate."

"I regret I do not have my rig standing by." Boyce regretted not having the blunt to hire the job horses that pulled his carriage. As soon as the betrothal was announced. . . . "But the woman might recover with a rest, as she says."

Ruthie was nodding. Torrie was undecided—until she saw a tall, bare-headed figure coming up the path behind an older couple. She turned to Boyce. "Very well, sir, I will be pleased to accept your escort for a short stroll."

Lord Boyce had trouble keeping up with her, she was walking so fast. His corset was too tight and his boots were more fashionable than well-fitting. Besides, they were going in the wrong direction. How could he hope to compromise a female when there was no one to see her fall from grace? The maid did not count, for she would be loyal to whatever her mistress wished her to say. Boyce did not have enough of the ready to bribe her to say Lady Torrie had given her virtue to him in the park.

If he had to, he could pull the earl's daughter behind a bush and rip her clothing. Lady Torrie would be forced to wed him after indulging in what everyone would believe was a passionate tryst. But his own clothing might become disordered in the struggle. Besides, the strong-willed female was just as liable to complain of being attacked. Her father would horsewhip him.

No, his first plan was better: one kiss, suitably passionate, in front of witnesses, then a declaration. While she was too stunned to challenge him, Boyce would say that he had been overcome with emotion when his beloved accepted his proposal. If she denied the engagement, her reputation would be in tatters for allowing such liberties in so public a venue. He thought he ought to put his hand on her breast to guarantee her disgrace. With his gloves on or off?

Torrie wanted to walk down a side path, behind the bench where Ruthie sat. Boyce wished to head back toward the entrance, where the riders gathered before setting out and knots of people gathered, no matter what the hour. He pulled toward the left. She pulled toward the right.

"But I saw a particularly attractive bird in this direction," Boyce said.

But Torrie saw a particular dog darting among the shrubbery where he was pointing. She tugged on Boyce's arm, hard enough to wrinkle his sleeve.

"Very well, my dear. We will walk this way." His lordship considered himself too much the gentleman to wrench a wench's arm, but he was too needy to let go. He'd just have to hope that the elderly couple who walked toward them on the path were of enough consequence to blacken her name sufficiently, finding her in *flagrante delicto*. Or as flagrant as one could get in one's clothes, in the park, in a hurry.

He let her lead him off the main walkway, but then he stopped as if to admire a flower, to let the couple catch up. Instead they seemed to get into some kind of altercation with another man who had come up the path, the same lout whose dog had misbehaved earlier. Botheration.

Needing to delay, Boyce decided to give his chosen bride one last chance to choose him.

"Lady Torrie," he began, then decided the occasion required a more formal form of address—before he tore her dress, if necessary. "Lady Victoria, you must know how much I admire you. Your beauty and your spirit are the epitome of womanhood. Your very smile can bring the strongest man to his knees." Of course not on the dirt, no matter the protocol. "I must beg you again to make me the happiest of men."

Torrie was looking back toward her maid, trying to figure out what was happening. The elderly man was shouting, waving his cane, and the woman was pointing with her parasol to where the dog was running off with a sack of something in his mouth. Oh, dear. The man started flailing ineffectively at Lord Ingall with his cane, and Torrie could not help the smile that came to her lips. She'd like to give the viscount a few good raps herself. "Yes!"

"Then you will?" Boyce almost fell backward in shock.

"Will what?" Torrie asked, turning back to him.

"Marry me, of course."

"Don't be more foolish than you need, George. I have told you endlessly that I shall never wed you. I shall not change my mind."

"Oh yes, you shall, my fine lady." And he grabbed for her.

Torrie was so surprised that she did not resist for a moment, until she felt his mouth on hers, and his tongue trying to force itself past her lips. She could not decide whether to employ her knee, her fist, or the tiny gun her father had insisted she carry in her reticule. When she felt his hand on her breast, she decided on all three, in whichever order they came. Before she could draw back her arm, or raise her leg, though, Lord Boyce was flying through the air, headfirst, into a newly planted border garden.

Boyce picked his head up out of the primroses, which he could not tell from parsley, and moaned.

His plan was ruined.

His clothes were ruined.

And a filthy mongrel was mangling the tassels on his boots.

Chapter Fourteen

Boyce spit out a leaf, and then he spit out: "You!"
His attacker had been the same busybody who had
foiled Boyce's attempt to look the hero in Lady Torrie's
eyes: Ingall. The same reprobate who should have been
driven out of London. The same no-account who . . .

"Yes, it is I." Wynn really wished he had bought himself one of those quizzing glasses, like the one broken
in Boyce's fall. He could have brought it to his eye and
scrutinized the maggot like the insect he was. If he ever
found a proper valet, Wynn swore, he'd send the fellow
out to purchase one. Meantime, he raised one eyebrow
and said, "And I am enjoying the coincidence of our
meeting again as little as you are, I am certain."

Boyce, however, was the one struggling to his feet
while Ingall did not seem the least discomposed.

"How dare you! I'll call you out for this, sirrah!"

"Save your breath, Boyce. You are already looking
apoplectic. And I will not duel you or anyone else."

Boyce curled his lip. "Of course. Dueling is for gentlemen, and you no longer classify as such, I recall."

"While you are refreshing your memory, you might
remember that the last man who challenged me is worm-
fodder. My aim has only improved, of necessity. Wolves,
crocodiles, and man-eating tigers, you know, do wonders
for sharpening one's marksmanship."

Now that was a hint Boyce did recognize. He brushed

down his floral-embroidered waistcoat and conceded, "Well, I do not suppose any harm has been done."

Wynn turned to Torrie. "I think that is for the lady to decide."

Torrie was mortified. To be found in such an undignified situation, by this of all people, was outside of enough. "I can explain," she began.

The viscount held up his hand. "I do not need to hear your explanation, my lady. I, for one, assume there is a good reason that a young woman would amble off alone with a rejected suitor." Left unsaid was her own earlier, unspoken, rush to judgment.

Boyce decided to make one last effort. "Rejected? Why, it is no such thing! Lady Victoria has accepted my suit. I fear my joy overcame my good manners. If you had not so rudely interrupted, we—"

"Stubble it," Torrie said, borrowing one of her father's favorite expressions. "You know it was no such thing."

Wynn reached down to take a tassel out of Homer's mouth. He tossed it at Boyce. "You heard the lady. There is no betrothal, and there better not be a repeat of this incident. Nor, I might mention, had there better be word of it stirred into this day's portion of scandal broth."

"There will not be," Torrie assured him. "Think how badly the scene reflects on Lord Boyce, and he would be the only one to speak of it in public. I certainly shall not. Will you, Lord Ingall?"

Wynn shook his head. What, and drag a lady's name through the mud the way Homer was dragging Boyce's walking stick? Was that how poorly she thought of him now? He whistled for the dog. "You should be getting back to your maid. She will be worrying over the delay."

"Heavens, poor Ruthie, and her not feeling well. I knew I should not have gone and left her!" Without a second glance to Boyce, she turned and headed back toward the main path where the bench was.

Wynn walked beside her, easily matching her hurried strides.

"Your escort is not necessary, sir. I am certain your own companion—"

"—has left the park. I will see you back to the bench, and then walk you and your woman to your carriage or a hackney."

He had neither asked nor offered, Torrie noted, simply issued an edict. "You need not concern yourself. Unless you think the park is littered with importunate suitors."

"I think it is populated by squirrels, pigeons, and pea hens who do not recognize danger until it jumps out at them."

Well, she would not have gone off with Boyce in the first place if she had not wanted to avoid Lord Ingall, but Torrie did not say so. Instead she took her ivory-handled pistol from her reticule. "I am not as foolish as you seem to believe. I realize that I owe you another debt of gratitude for coming to my rescue once again, but the situation was not nearly so dire on this occasion. I would have managed."

He looked at the pretty but adequate weapon. "Tell me, my lady, could you have shot Boyce? Could you have put the muzzle of your little gun against his heart and pulled the trigger?"

"I . . . I am not certain. If he was intent on doing me harm, I suppose. But for taking liberties?"

Wynn believed the dastard was intent on taking a great deal more than a few kisses, but he saw no need to frighten her needlessly with unfounded suspicions. He did take the gun from her with one flick of his wrist to prove his point. He put it in his pocket, after checking to make sure it was not cocked. The gudgeon could have shot her own foot off— or worse. "You see how easily a man can disarm a smaller, weaker person? What would you have done had he turned the weapon on you, threatening you with bodily harm unless you agreed to his terms?"

"Lord Boyce? Now who is being foolish?"

"A desperate man can be the most dangerous. By all reports, Boyce has reached point non plus. He needs your dowry."

"Gammon. Boyce knows very well that my father would not let me be forced into any marriage against my will. I have only to say no in front of the vicar. Besides, Lord Boyce might be a boor, but he is a gentleman."

And Lady Torrie was still a naive ninnyhammer. A beautiful ninnyhammer, with eyes that were bluer than this April sky, but still a cabbage-head.

He had to show her that she was not invulnerable, despite being rich and titled and pluck to the backbone. She might be a game 'um, as they said, but she still needed a man to defend and protect her. Wynn felt it was his duty to expose her weaknesses, so she would be more careful in the future. That's what he told himself, anyway.

It was a good excuse for doing what he wanted, what Boyce had begun.

So he dragged her behind a small stand of trees.

"What are you doing? My maid—"

"Has waited this long."

So had Wynn. He pulled her closer. "Now, my lady, what would you do if Boyce did this?" He pinned her arms at her sides, loosely, without force, but with enough strength to show her she could not escape unless he let her. He bent her back slightly, then brought his mouth to hers.

Torrie knew he was trying to teach her a lesson, the arrogant jackass, but she was willing to learn a few facts about him—and his kisses—while he was at it. He did not grind his lips into hers as Boyce did, thank goodness. Instead, his lips felt . . .

She could not describe how they felt, cool and warm at the same time, soft and hard, giving yet taking. Just when she thought she might have a better understanding of the conundrum, he pulled back.

Torrie sighed.

"What if he did this?" Wynn asked, tenderly kissing her eyelids shut, then placing butterfly kisses on her cheeks and her neck.

Torrie sighed again.

One of his arms started stroking circles on her back, then her side, and then started circling higher, toward one of her breasts. "What if he did this?"

If Boyce's touch had felt like this, if he had made her feel like this, with every inch of her skin aching for his attention despite the layers of her spencer and gown and shift between them, she would have married him three years ago when he first asked. But this was not Boyce holding her so gently, so cherishingly, if such a word existed. If it did not, it should.

No, this was not Boyce. This was Ingall, Wynn, who would never hurt her or steal what she refused to give. Who made her feel like a flower unfurling, like a bird getting ready to fly. Who had saved her twice, saved her for him. She was sure of it. If the Fates had not meant them to be together, they would not fit so well together, their very breaths becoming one to share. She was where she was meant to be, by chance or by a grand design, and she meant to enjoy it.

Torrie leaned closer into his hand, into his hard body, into his lips, making little mews of pleasure that drove him to deepen the kiss.

"What," he whispered into her mouth, "if he did this?" His tongue followed the whisper, lightly touching her teeth, then her own tongue.

Torrie was on fire, and she could feel Wynn's answering heat, despite the layers of clothing between them. They were sure to leave scorched footprints in the grass where they stood. Everyone would know, and she did

not care. Torrie felt she would die if he went further—
and die if he stopped.

But then Wynn recalled where he was—and who he
was. No matter what the gossip-grinders murmured, no
matter what his body shouted, he was a gentleman. And
Torrie was a lady. He stepped back, although it may
have been the hardest thing he had ever done, to the
hardest he had ever been.

He said, "You see? Boyce could have had you on the
ground with your skirts up to your waist, without force."

He did not see at all, Torrie thought, if he believed
she turned into a smoldering ember for just any man.
Boyce could never have succeeded in benumbing her
defenses, not for one instant, much less long enough to
tumble her to the grass. Why, she would have boxed
Boyce's ears if he had taken one of the liberties Wynn
had. In honesty, she had to admit to herself that Wynn
had not so much taken liberties as he had been offered
them. Embarrassed, she remembered pressing herself
closer and closer to him, finding proof that he was as
enkindled as she had been.

Lud, did he think Boyce could do that to her? She
doubted even Boyce believed he could turn her into a
wanton. No, only Wynn could, or ever had, although she
doubted he had expected to be as affected. Her mind
might be addled, but she knew he had felt the fire, too,
will he or nill he.

What had started as a lesson, that she could never
defend herself against a bully, had turned into something
else altogether, until he recalled his priggish point. As if
she believed she could hold her own against a slavering
giant with a bat. Of course, she could not, no more than
he could, or one of her father's footmen. Were someone
bound on mayhem, with a knife or a rifle, say, none of
them stood a chance. But Wynn had thought to make
his argument with kisses, showing his superiority to her
bacon-brained bravado.

Well, she had a few points of her own to make:

She was not a schoolgirl he could kiss silly.

She was not a piece of Haymarket ware to be handled casually for a moment's pleasure and then tossed aside.

She was not one of his women.

So she kicked him, the way her father had taught her.

When Wynn recovered, Homer was licking his face, and Lady Torrie and her maid were long gone. Perhaps he should marry Rosie after all, he thought, for he might never have children of his own anyway. Then he sat up and took stock.

So far today he had promised to find a husband for a pregnant prostitute.

He had paid a fortune in reparations for his dog's transgressions.

And he had made a dangerous enemy. Perhaps two, although he doubted Torrie would hold a grudge the way Boyce would.

Not a bad morning's work, he told himself, and it was not even noon. He brushed himself off and started to head toward home, the dog at his side.

Oh, he recalled with a smile, and he had kissed Torrie Keyes. He had not done too poorly for a simple walk in the park, not at all.

Chapter Fifteen

Lord, she had kicked a man! A gentleman, who had been nothing but noble toward her. Torrie was mortified. She could have punched Wynn—she had long since stopped thinking of him as Lord Ingall; the kiss was far too personal for titled formality—instead. That was what she should have done, for her father had also taught her all about closed fists and where to aim. But the viscount's nose was already somewhat less than perfect. If she had managed to smash it, he would begin to look like that ugly little man she had seen around Grosvenor Square a few times recently.

Lord, she had kissed a man! And what a man! What a kiss! Of course, as Aunt Ann would have said, being a proficient lover had to be a rake's stock in trade. If Lord Ingall had been intent on seduction, though, he was right: he could indeed have accomplished it handily—the hand on her breast, the hand stroking her back. But he hadn't. He didn't. He wasn't. A rake, that is.

Torrie was absolutely convinced that there was a rational, respectable reason for that scene with the burgeoning barque of frailty, just as Wynn had reserved judgment about her encounter with Boyce. He had not implied by word or expression the least condemnation of her morals, only a criticism of her intelligence in walking off with Boyce.

Even her father, when he heard an extremely expurgated account of the day's events, demanded that she henceforth take a footman with her wherever she went. Torrie would not have mentioned the contretemps with Boyce at all except that Ruthie had seen her go off with him, and come back without him. Torrie had still been so agitated when they arrived home that she'd had to say something. She did not repeat Wynn's suspicions that Lord Boyce was set on compromising her, lest her father forbid her to leave the house, nor did she cite Wynn's kiss, lest her father forbid him to call at the house. She merely said that he had rescued her, again, from an uncomfortable encounter. The earl was all for inviting him to dinner, again.

"What, and have him think my niece is pursuing him like a hound on a scent?" Aunt Ann stabbed her needle through the fabric of yet another footstool cover. "Do not be a clunch, brother. We already have him escorting us to Mrs. Reese's affair next week. Any other invitations would smack of the hunt. Nothing will make a man like Ingall run faster in the other direction."

"Heavens, Aunt, you make it sound as though I am out to snabble the poor man against his will."

"Aren't you? All this talk about Fate and bargaining for your life, I swear you will be reading the tea leaves next, or casting love spells. Though what you want with a man like that I cannot imagine."

That was because Aunt Ann had never been kissed like that, by a man like that. Or by any man, perhaps. Wynn might not be an easy husband but, heavens, he would be an exciting one. Torrie fingered the key amulet she wore at her neck. She thought her own heart's portal could be easily breached, but had she begun to unlock his at all? Time would tell, time she meant to put to good use. If that kiss had not opened his heart, the gown she intended to have made for Mrs. Reese's ball would definitely rattle its gates.

Torrie still needed a new habit, the green velvet she had selected at Madame Michaela's having been destroyed by the fire brigade's zeal in wetting down the entire shop. The mantua-maker had been fortunate enough to locate an empty store nearby and was moving her operation there, with the financial assistance of an anonymous donor. Torrie thought she should help the business recover by renewing her order—and adding one for a new ball gown. There might not be as much choice of fabric or trim in the hastily restocked store, but the gown Torrie envisioned required little of either.

Her fashionable mother would have known precisely what Torrie had in mind. Her perpetually black-clad aunt would not have the least idea. Ruthie might have been a help in selecting a pattern and material, but Torrie felt her maid should stay home and rest.

The doctor had been called, at Torrie's insistence, because Ruthie had been ailing too long. When the Keyes's usual physician heard that he was to attend a mere maid, however, he declared himself too busy and sent his assistant instead. The assistant instantly and enthusiastically prescribed his favorite stomach powders—the same powders he recommended for the Munson's chef, who was too fond of his own cooking wines, and for Lady Wilsted's dyspeptic poodle.

Ruthie seemed a bit improved, but Torrie did not think a new gown, even one so crucial, was worth chancing a setback for. She left her maid home in the care of the housekeeper and took one of the footmen instead. Henry would be useless at picking styles, but his presence would make her father happy. The gown Torrie meant to have would not.

How the devil had he come to kiss Lady Torrie? Damn, Wynn was still thinking the next day, how the devil had he waited so long? Now he was going to want to do it again—and he'd be hanged before he did. He might be hanged if he did, if Lord Duchamp got wind of it. He was no uncivilized beast, though, acting on his every urge, despite the incident in the park. He'd had provocation then: another man kissing her. So he had

hurled Boyce to the ground, dragged the woman behind
a bush, and proceeded to have his way with her. Now
that was civilized.

Bah!

Well, he swore, it would not happen again. To be certain, he would simply stay away from her. That ball of
Mrs. Reese's was looming nearer, but that would be the
end of it. He never had to see the earl's daughter after-
ward. He never had to be so tempted again.

To be sure, he refused the invitations that had arrived
in force after the dinner at Duchamp House. Oddly, no
new ones had arrived in the days since. According to
Barrogi, who spent his free time, which Wynn suspected
was most of his time, at various pubs frequented by the
serving class, the *ton* did not know what to make of
Viscount Ingall. On the one hand, he was rich and titled
and Lady Torrie's hero. On the other, he was suspected
of killing a fellow peer.

The young bucks and blades were trying to tie his
Bundler neckcloth, but the biddy hens were clacking
their beaks. Someone, and neither Barrogi nor Wynn
doubted it was Lord Boyce, was raking up the coals of
the old scandal. Now there were added whispers that
Wynn had shot early at the duel. No one had witnessed
the fatal event except the combatants, one of whom was
dead, and the seconds, one of whom was dead, and the
surgeon, who had disappeared. No one, therefore,
could—or would—refute the murmured charges.

Wynn's second had been his boyhood friend, Troy,
the one who had given Wynn his life's savings before
going off to the army, never to return. Lynbrook's second had been his younger brother Francis, who had been
all too eager to step into the baron's boots.

"There is more gossip making the rounds, *padrone*,"
Barrogi reported, "about how that fire was suspicious,
sí, and you just happened to be passing by."

"Deuce take it, hundreds of people must have passed
by that shop that day!"

"*Sí, padrone*, but most have not been battening on Duchamp's gratitude."

"Battening? I have never battened on anyone in my life!"

Barrogi hunched his shoulders. "Who is to say, when the *signore*, he is putting your name up for a government post and membership in his clubs? And when you accosted the emerald in the park?"

"The Diamond. They call Lady Torrie the Keyes Diamond because she is so priceless and she wears that little charm around her neck, a diamond key. And I would never—" Well, he had, but only after Boyce had. "Boyce." He spoke the name like a foul epithet. "This is just like that maggot, to fight a man with innuendo instead of with his fists, to tell lies behind his back. I should have broken his scrawny neck while I had the chance."

The stiletto suddenly appeared in Barrogi's gnarled hand. "You want I should stop him? A man with no tongue cannot sing."

"Good heavens, man, put that thing away. Just find the dastard who set the fire. He should lead us back to Boyce, with a little convincing. With money, not your knife! We are in England now, not the Barbary Coast."

They were in England, all right, where the rich and powerful had nothing to do except slander each other. It was just like last time, when they were so ready to condemn him on a few hints of wrongdoing. But it was not precisely like six years ago.

Now Wynn was rich and powerful.

Now he did not care what anyone thought of him.

And now he was not going to run.

Let them think the worst and let them close their doors. He did not want to step over their thresholds anyway. What, to drink watered wine and stale cakes? He would not mind if Mrs. Reese rescinded her invitation, for then he would not have to suffer through a blasted ball with its simpering misses and avaricious mamas. So let the high sticklers turn him away. He had plenty of other places where he'd be welcomed.

Not his own home, of course. Not with his sister-in-law Marissa in residence at Ingram House.

Not Duchamp House, perhaps, not after his astounding breach of etiquette in the park yesterday.

Not at Rosie's flat, not until he found her a husband.

Which left calling on Bette, Lady Lynbrook. He could not visit the woman whose husband he was purported to have killed looking like a buccaneer, though. He had sticking plaster on his chin from shaving, a torn sleeve on his new coat from tossing Boyce, and no tassels on his boots, from Homer having acquired a new hobby. He needed a valet.

Barrogi found a handful of likely candidates at Shay's Tavern, a pub where returned soldiers gathered, when they could afford the price of a pint. Too many were too foxed to be considered, but three came for interviews. The first man had only one hand.

Barrogi shrugged. "You have only one neck, *padrone*."

The second fellow wore a string of small bones, perhaps human knuckle bones, atop his frayed uniform collar. Wynn did not want to count the number of dead, fingerless Frenchmen. Nor did he want to consider sleeping in the next room to a man who collected such trophies.

The third man looked like he had not shaved in years. With whiskers, mustache, and sideburns, he looked like a veritable orangutan Wynn had seen once. Lud, the man was so out of practice Wynn was like to have his throat cut.

None would do. He did send the first two on to his Hertfordshire estate steward, where old Bimm could find work for any number of willing hands, even if they were a hand short. The bone-collector might find a position with the butcher. The hirsute man he hired to help keep watch over Lady Torrie, when Barrogi was busy.

Then he had Barrogi buy a round for the other veter-

ans at Shay's. A round of cheese, that is, and around a
dozen steak and kidney pasties from the pieman at the
corner. Heaven knew the government was not going to
feed these poor sots who had fought so hard for their
country.

He still needed a valet.

"You want I should find the arsonist, *padrone*, or find
you *un servitore* to powder your arse?"

"I can't do any worse than you at finding a gentleman's gentleman." Wynn spoke in scathing tones, re-
senting his hired man's inference that he could not dress
himself. Of course he could, and had for years, just not
up to Lady Torrie's—to London's—standards. "You
work on the fire starter. Oh, and look in on Rosie. Make
sure she does not need anything. She could use the
company."

Barrogi nodded. "The *signora* is lonely."

Wynn sighed. "She is a *signorina,* I am afraid. That is
the problem." And she'd had one too many companions.

The older man shook his head and insisted on *signora*.
"For respect, even though she cheats at cards."

Wynn was not surprised Rosie had invited Barrogi up
to her rooms after their ices at Gunter's, she was that
bored. Neither was he surprised she had cheated. "Of
course she knows every crooked trick in the game.
That's how she got so far. The house always wins, you
know."

Barrogi flashed his gap-toothed grin and his own deck
of shaved and marked cards. "Not today. Today the
house has lice."

"Loses?"

"But of course."

Chapter Sixteen

"You came! Oh, Wynn, you came!" Bette, Lady Lynbrook threw herself into Wynn's arms and proceeded to rumple his last decent shirt. Her face was buried so deeply in his chest he could not even get a good look at her, to see if his old playmate had changed much in the six years since he had been gone. She sure as Hades had not changed from the overwrought and overemotional little baggage she had always been.

"Give over, Bette. I wrote and said I would come."

She sniffled into his striped waistcoat. "That was weeks ago."

"It was days. And I am here now, so stop crying and tell me how you have been. Your letters were so tear-stained I could barely make out the words." He had given up at the third mention of the word "marriage."

"Oh, Wynn, things have been so awful here. You cannot imagine."

He looked around at the elegant luxury of Lynbrook House, glad he had left Homer in Kensington, and no, he could not imagine what had her so agitated, not after the places he had been forced to call home. From the cushiony softness in his arms, he knew she had been getting enough to eat. Ample food and shelter would have seemed like paradise to him, some days of his travels. "Why don't you sit and tell me."

She finally released him, leading the way to a sunny breakfast parlor, where she called for tea and cakes.

While they waited for the servants to finish laying out the light repast, Wynn had time for a good look at Bette, who was the younger dowager Lady Lynbrook, since her deceased husband's mother still lived, and the current baron had a Lady Lynbrook of his own.

Bette used to be Bette Dodge when he spent his summer holidays at his friend Troy's home in the Lake District, the eldest daughter of a prosperous family. Her parents had the neighboring estate, and the three youngsters spent many hours together. Bette was not permitted to accompany the boys when they went shooting or fishing or swimming, of course, but there were long hikes and sketching expeditions, and merry games in her family's parlor, all things Wynn had not known at his own house. He took every invitation offered to vacation at Troy Campe's, and his own parents never cared enough to miss him.

Bette and Troy had known each other since the cradle, and both they and Wynn assumed the two would wed one day. But Bette's parents had higher ambitions than the squire's second son, who was meant for a career in the army. They promised her to Frederick, Lord Lynbrook, a rum go, but a baron. Bette acquired a title, Troy acquired his colors, and Wynn set out to acquire town bronze.

Then came Lynbrook's drunken rages, the duel, and Ciudad Rodrigo. All of their lives had changed.

Some few years away from her thirtieth birthday—but more years past her twentieth—Bette was still a fetching little buttercup, although Wynn suspected some of the blond color came from a bottle. She had put on more than a few pounds since her widowhood, but they, and the scrap of a lace cap she wore, were the only signs of a fleeting youth. She still had her dimpled chin, and she still pouted when tears did not work to get her way. She was pouting now.

"I told you how it was, how Frederick's brother Francis keeps me in near penury. I cannot afford to travel, not even to Bath or Brighton. I could not entertain here, if I had any friends, for the place has grown so shabby, but Francis will not release the funds to refurbish it since he spends most of his time in the country. He says he needs the money for Three Brooks, but I know he maintains a cottage nearby for his mistresses. I'd wager that cottage is in better condition than this old pile."

The house looked fine to Wynn, especially after his lodgings in Kensington, but he admitted he knew little of current decorating trends. Bette was going on with her list of woes anyway: her wardrobe was threadbare and dated; her jewels were claimed by Francis for his own wife, Angela; and all of the family vehicles and most of the servants were gone north to Three Brooks with the family for Angela's latest lying-in.

"Then why did you not go with them?" Wynn asked, thinking it was a reasonable question, not a call for more tears. "You would be more comfortable without spending your own funds, and have more companionship."

Her handkerchief was already sodden, so he handed over his. "Francis refuses to allow me my own household, so my only company would be Frederick's mother in the Dower House, and she hates me! She blames me—and you, of course—for Frederick's death. I cannot go there! No, nor to my family home, either. My parents say I would be a bad influence on my younger sisters, what with the scandal and all. Two of them remain to be wed, you understand."

"Surely you have friends in town, young women who made their come-outs with you who never married. Or another widow living in somewhat straitened circumstances also. If you pool your resources . . ."

"I have no friends!" she cried, only muffled somewhat by his handkerchief. "No one receives me except the fast crowd, and I cannot afford their company. Francis refuses to pay my gambling debts."

"Well, I cannot say as I blame him there, Bette. With a growing family—"

"He is a miser, I tell you. A lick-penny, a cheese-parer, and a cheat. I swear my marriage settlements should have yielded more income, but he says the monies were invested in the Funds, and lost value. I know he spends lavishly on his high flyers, because the bills sometimes come here in error."

"And you open them, of course."

"How else am I supposed to know how he is spending my money?"

Wynn never had trusted Lynbrook's younger brother. Now he had more reasons. "I will have my man of business look into it."

"What good will that do me? I will still be old and ugly and all alone in the world. Oh, what is to become of me?" She raised one hand to her brow and sobbed.

"Well, you could take up a career on the stage, for all your histrionics. Now, blow your nose like a good girl and tell me what you really want from me."

"I do not want to be a dowager, Wynn."

"That is easy. Get remarried."

"Which is precisely the solution I arrived at. The only problem is, I have no dowry, I never conceived in the years of my marriage so I might be barren, and"—here a note of accusation mingled with the whine—"my reputation was destroyed by that duel."

Not as much as Wynn's reputation was ruined, he'd wager. "But you are still an incomparable, Bette. Surely there is some man who would be happy to have you gracing his be—that is, his dinner table."

"Would you?"

The room was suddenly five degrees warmer. Wynn wished for his handkerchief back so he could wipe his brow. "I, um, I . . ."

"You helped me before."

They had decided that Wynn had to be the one to challenge Lynbrook. Troy would have lost his commission for breaking one of Wellesley's prime rules against his officers dueling. Besides, Wynn was a better shot.

"Well, yes, we were old friends. We could not let that swine continue abusing you. But that is not to say . . . marriage."

"Why not? We would suit perfectly. And that way I would have my reputation back, since a marriage would satisfy the old tabbies with a romantical happy ending. Everyone knows you were my paramour, anyway."

"But I never was your lover, you gudgeon. You knew I was just flirting with you to make Frederick angry enough to accept the challenge."

"He was madder that you stole Rosie Peters from him."

"I did not steal Rosie, I bought her. Actually, I leased her temporarily, at her price, and that only to deflect gossip from you."

Bette waved the handkerchief in the air. "No one swallowed that taradiddle anyway. They all believed that you killed Frederick out of love for me."

"I did not kill Frederick."

"Of course you did. You shot him through the heart, which was not at all what Troy planned."

"I shot him in the shoulder."

"Oh, bosh. He would not have died of a ball in the shoulder. At least not for some time even if the wound turned putrid."

Wynn started drumming his fingers on the chair's armrest, to release some of his own pent-up emotions. "Bette, I say again, I aimed at the loose screw's shoulder." He paused. "And I do not miss my target."

"But they told me . . . I saw . . ."

"He walked to his damned carriage! A man with a fatal wound could not do that, could he? I have no idea what happened, but I have my suspicions. If you did not kill him—"

She shrieked. "Me? You think I killed my husband?"

Wynn glanced to make sure the door was securely closed. "Why not? He was unfaithful and violent toward you. My shot, nay, the whole duel, was a warning, but

Lynbrook would have lived. You might easily have taken the opportunity to find a more permanent solution while he was unconscious."

"You spent six years thinking I killed Lynbrook? No wonder you did not wish to marry me. But now . . ."

"You spent the same six years thinking I had killed a man, almost in cold blood, so one can only wonder why you would marry me. My fortune would have nothing to do with your sudden attraction, would it?"

"Oh, you are hateful." She started weeping again. "I always knew I should have married Troy."

"What, and follow the drum?" Wynn couldn't think of a woman less likely to survive the rigors of army life. Lady Torrie could manage, with her wit and courage, but Bette? She would not last a week, and then only if no one strangled her to stop her whining. "Your parents would never have given permission."

"We could have eloped. Troy did not wish to, but I could have convinced him."

"A Gretna Green ceremony would still have been a scandal, and you would still be a widow."

"But I would have a beautiful memory to cherish as my teeth fall out and my hearing fails and my chin droops. I would have known some love in my life."

Wynn felt a pain in the vicinity of his heart at Bette's words. It must be the almond cakes. He cleared his throat. "You are still young. There is time."

"No, there is not," she bawled. "I am already getting fat, and I swear I saw a gray hair. No one will ever want me again."

With that she launched herself off her sofa and onto his lap in a leap that would have done Homer proud. Wynn checked that door again. He would not put it past this household to be setting another trap for him, this one ready to claim compromise. If he heard the softest footstep approach the door, he'd dump Bette on the floor so fast her hair might truly turn silver. At least her added poundage would cushion her fall. In the meantime, while she wept into the wad he was calling a neck-cloth these days, he was thinking that he did not feel the slightest urge to hold her closer, or to kiss away her tears, or touch that smooth skin on the back of her neck. Unlike any time he was in the vicinity of Lady Torrie, he felt absolutely nothing, except sore muscles from Bette's weight. He did have an idea, however.

"Bette, my dear, I have a question to put to you."

She sighed and stopped crying and adjusted the lace cap on her head. "I knew you would not let me down, Wynn. You were always a good and loyal friend. Yes."

"Yes, what?"

"Yes, in answer to your question."

"Oh, then you do know where I can find Frederick's valet."

Chapter Seventeen

In the end, they went shopping. That was the fastest, surest way Wynn knew to stop Bette's tears, other than offering to marry her. He'd buy out every shop in London first. Hell, he *buy* every shop in London first.

As Wynn explained to Lady Lynbrook along the way, he was making a start toward respectability without half trying. A wealthy, titled bachelor did not have to try as hard, say, as a flighty young widow with a murky reputation. Wynn did not care about his reception for himself, but as soon as he was socially acceptable, he could see about invitations for Bette. He could even act as her escort to proper, dignified occasions at the finer homes, where they would behave so circumspectly toward each other that the cackling gossip would have to look elsewhere for a roost. Bette could find a husband in a wink—if she was rigged out in style. Nothing would ruin her chances faster than looking fast, which were the only styles that appealed to the baroness, or like someone's cast-off, which was how her out-of-fashion, slightly puckered gowns appeared to Wynn.

In a way Wynn felt like a traitor to his sex, trying to dress Lynbrook's little mutton as lamb, to bait parson's mousetrap. But, dash it, if he could not find Bette a husband, Wynn knew he'd have her on his hands, in his lap, sobbing on his shirtfront, forever. Better some knocked-in-the-cradle cawker than him.

No one could know Wynn was paying her bills, of

course. That would sink the widow's chances of receiving anything but highly improper proposals and invitations to the wilder sort of parties. The latter might be more fun than staid musicales, but they would never yield up a husband.

Luckily, Wynn knew just the place to take Bette for her new apparel, a shop that was barely open, so would not be busy, and where the dressmaker was so grateful she would never discuss his business nor divulge his secrets. All he had to do was put Lady Lynbrook in Madame Michaela's capable hands, then he could leave for an hour or two. Or three. If Michaela was the mantuamaker who had the dressing of Lady Torrie, she was more than capable of outfitting Bette, although, he thought, Lady Torrie would look superb in anything. And better in nothing.

"Heavens, Wynn, you almost tripped me," Bette complained. "Do pay attention to where you are going."

Torrie was in the fitting room with *madame*'s assistant, Tina. All of the modiste's notes and measurements were lost in the fire and had to be retaken, a tedious business made slower by Torrie's indecision regarding the neckline of her new gown. Too high and she would look like every other young female on the Marriage Mart. Too low and she would look like a Cyprian. Somewhere in the middle had to be the perfect spot to strike a certain eye, if the gold tissue she had selected did not catch his interest.

Happily, he had sent a note with another bouquet of violets, apologizing for his forward actions in the park and begging her to forget the incident. She had sent back a reply apologizing for her own behavior, and requesting he, in turn, forget. He must have forgotten her altogether, for Torrie had not seen hide nor hair of the viscount since. Well, she promised herself, he would not forget her in the gown she would wear to Mrs. Reese's benefit ball.

"A smidgen lower," she ordered Tina.

The bell at the front door jangled, and she could hear Madame Michaela greet a new customer. In fact, she could hear every word.

"*Monsieur,* what a pleasure. I was hoping you would come so I could thank you again, and again. What would I do without your generosity, your kindness? I tell you, my girls and I would be out on the street, hemming handkerchiefs for ha'pennies. You are my savior, my *chevalier tres gallant.*" In case he could not understand her French accent, the dressmaker added, "My hero. Why, you—"

"Please, *madame,* no more," Torrie heard a familiar voice say. So he had been the one who helped the seamstress! She smiled to herself, warmed by the thought of his goodness. Then he said, "I have come to beg a favor from you."

"For you, *monsieur,* anything."

"My friend needs a new wardrobe."

The smile faded from Torrie's lips. His friend?

"I can see that. I mean *oui.* It shall be my pleasure."

"She will need some of the gowns as soon as possible."

"For your friend, nothing is impossible."

She had told Torrie her new gown would cost an additional fortune, to be ready in time, since the seamstresses were having to remake half of the previous orders.

"I will pay for the extra effort, of course."

He would pay? Ingall had not said it was his sister or his cousin who needed a new wardrobe, but his friend. No man bought a friend's clothing. He bought her a book or a fan, for heaven's sake. And no respectable woman accepted more than a pair of gloves from a gentleman. Yet he was going on about the gowns to be selected, how they had to be modest without being moppish, and modish without being daring. In other words, respectable. Torrie wished she could get a good look at the woman, who was giggling now, but she did not want to seem too interested in front of Tina, and she most definitely did not want to be seen by Lord Ingall and his *cherie amie*.

"Fine," he was saying in response to *madame*'s sugges- tions. "I see that you understand perfectly. I am confi- dent I can leave Lady Lynbrook in your expert and efficient hands."

Lady Lynbrook? Torrie turned around so fast the measuring tape flew out of Tina's hands. His former mis- tress? His *other* former mistress? Between the baroness and the faro dealer, it was no wonder the man had not had time to call on her! And he was purchasing this one a new gown. No, a new wardrobe. And he had kissed Torrie in the park, the lewd, licentious lecher. She only wished she'd kicked him harder.

Then she heard the doorbell jangle as he left, and she took a deep breath. She was doing it again, rushing to judgment without knowing all the facts. Perhaps there was some explanation, as there had been when she was in Boyce's embrace. She had to give Lord Ingall the benefit of the doubt, she told herself, but doubts were making furrows on her brow. She could not think of a single instance where a single man could pay a woman's way that was not suspect, unless, of course, they were engaged to be wed.

Maybe Wynn had truly loved the lady all these years. After killing her husband, he must have deemed himself unworthy of her. While she had fallen into a decline, and into penury, he had waited to return until he had proved himself, to lay his heart and his fortune at her feet. Now they could finally plight their troth. No, that was the plot of the novel Torrie had sent her footman to return to the lending library while she had her fitting. Besides, she had not read any notice of the betrothal in the newspapers.

"Lower the neckline another inch, Tina."

When Wynn arrived at his lodgings in Kensington, a liveried messenger, not a written message, was waiting.

The servant's uniform colors looked more than familiar, dash it. The dark blue and gold were his own colors, his family colors. His sister-in-law, it seemed, had grown weary of waiting for Wynn's formal arrival.

Lady Ingall, the footman carefully recited, respectfully requested Lord Ingall's presence for dinner at Ingram House preceding the theater that evening.

Respectfully, like Hades. It was more of an order than an invitation, but Wynn was of a mind to accept. He would have to face Marissa soon enough anyway, if he ever wanted to get his town house, his signet ring, or his uniformed servants back. As head of the family, such as it was, he was aware that he had not paid Marissa her proper courtesies. Her frequent letters had reminded him of his dereliction from duty.

He might as well get the unpleasant chore over with. Besides, Marissa could not lecture him during the play, nor during the meal with the servants in the room, which left only the brief, before-dinner gathering for his sister-in-law to go off on her rant about duty and decency and dear Roger, who'd died of a stroke during a speech in Parliament. Wynn reasoned that he could arrive close enough to the dinner hour to shorten the diatribe considerably. She might just forget that bit about him delivering an heir for the viscountcy. Or pigs could fly. His attendance might soften Marissa's attitude toward him. Or pigs could fly upside down.

But she might prove handy, anyway. Marissa had been a political hostess, a doyenne of society before Wynn's brother's demise, and he doubted she had given up that power any more than she had given up Ingram House. He thought she could be of great assistance in bringing Bette back into society, if she consented to help. Or pigs could fly upside down on the backs of camels.

Still, Wynn had always enjoyed the theater. He thought he might enjoy an evening of high drama where he, for once, was not in a leading role. He could sit back and lose himself in someone else's tragedy, forgetting for the nonce his need to find a husband for Rosie, his vow to find a husband for Bette, and his instinct to keep Lady Torrie from finding any husband whatsoever, Boyce or otherwise. Watching Romeo and Juliet enact their imbecile infatuation was preferable to examining his own thoughts.

She would likely be at the theater that evening, too. Not Juliet—he had no idea what was being performed this evening—but Lady Torrie. Most of the *ton* attended the plays, he knew, arrayed in all their finery. Seeing the earl's daughter's finest would be well worth the price of one of Marissa's bear garden jaws.

He told the footman to report his acceptance. The servant looked surprised that Wynn considered he had a choice, but he bowed and left.

Now all Wynn had to do was prepare himself to endure Marissa's lectures, ignore her encroachments, and attire himself according to her exacting standards. Fortunately, the message to Lord Lynbrook's former valet had brought immediate results: Edsall. The baron's man was tall and thin, with skin so white he looked as if he had been interred in the crypt along with his deceased employer all these years. He smelled like it, too, as if he had been preserved in spirits. He stuttered and shook and would not meet Wynn's eyes. How the deuce was Edsall supposed to shave him, Wynn wondered, if he wouldn't look at him? Then he noticed the man's knobby knees were knocking together. Confound it, the man was afraid of—Homer? No, the dog was wagging his tail and the valet was paying him no attention. Barrogi was not even around, nor had he left his stiletto in sight, so that left Wynn himself. The mawworm was afraid of him! Likely he'd spent the afternoon drinking, just to give himself courage enough to face Lynbrook's killer. Thunderation.

Wynn sent Edsall away before the man fainted. He might have lowered himself to the milksop's expectations by holding a gun to his head until Edsall tied a proper neckcloth, but the man might have done what Homer did when terrified. Besides, Wynn had taken precautions against just such an eventuality as finding himself with no valet, again or still. He'd had Madame Michaela fashion an elegant knot for him, one with tapes that would tie around his neck under his shirt collar.

It was up to Marissa's standards.

It was easy enough for Wynn to attach by himself.

And it was in a hatbox in the corner—where Homer was making himself a comfortable nest of the snowy linen.

"I see you are still as rackety as ever, Ingall," was Marissa's greeting when the butler showed Wynn into the drawing room.

Chapter Eighteen

It was his house. His butler. And his best attempt at an Oriental. Even if it looked like an Accidental, Marissa should not have said anything. Not that manners, breeding, or minding her own business had ever mattered to Wynn's sister-in-law. It was she, more than anyone else, who thought his wild ways would reflect badly on his brother Roger's political career. It was she who convinced Wynn's father to ship him out of the country, rather than fight the charges and the slander.

"And a pleasant evening to you, also, Marissa. You are looking well." She had never looked good, but now she had a certain matronly dignity about her. She wore black, although Roger had been dead for over a year, but tempered the mourning with white lace trim and a long string of—his mother's—pearls. She still had a squint, which meant she was still too vain to wear spectacles.

Despite her poor vision, she obviously judged Wynn lacking. She sniffed, extended two bony fingers for his obligatory salute, and said, "I see I shall have to send Redding to you."

Since Redding was Roger's old valet, Wynn could forgive Marissa a great deal. He actually held her hand for longer than he would have held a dead trout. "I would be grateful," he said in all honesty.

As soon as Roger's widow had him settled on a crocodile-footed sofa in the Egyptian Room with a glass of wine, she wasted no time before cataloguing his sins, and enumerating her solutions. Wynn barely listened, too busy looking around. They had never had an Egyptian Room when he lived here. He doubted an Egyptian ever had a room quite like this, either, with jackal gods as table pedestals, hieroglyph-decorated pots of papyrus, and a sarcophagus propped in the corner against the green-painted wall.

Wynn was wondering how much this Nile-in-Mayfair had cost, who had paid for it, and why, when he was attacked by an asp. That is, Marissa had uttered the poisonous word he had been hearing all too often lately: marriage. Stung, Wynn forced himself to listen more closely.

Marissa, it seemed, considered matrimony the only way for Wynn to regain his respectability. No matter that he was not breeding like Rosie, nor considered fast and fallen like Bette, he was a disgrace, redeemable only by marriage to a woman above reproach. None of his harum-scarum harlots would do, Marissa insisted.

"And if you are thinking that flighty Keyes female will have you, save your breath. Duchamp does not need your money."

Wynn frowned, although Marissa could not see it. Confound it, he thought, Torrie was not flighty. She would have had him, for she'd asked. And no matter what Marissa believed, he had more to offer the right woman than merely money.

What Marissa believed—aside from thinking this museum monstrosity of a room was in any way comfortable—was that her cousin Deanna would suit him to a cow's thumb. Unless Marissa had the girl hidden in the sarcophagus, Wynn supposed he was expected to agree to the marriage sight unseen.

Deanna, Miss Herman, it appeared, was everything a man could wish for in a wife. "My cousin is well mannered and well favored, with no airs about her."

Marissa had enough pretensions for any one family.

"Her background is exceptional, of course, with titles on both sides of the family tree."

Wynn was reminded of Lord Duchamp's Irish stud. And of the old adage that if one did not like the stable, one ought not buy the filly.

Marissa continued: "Deanna is familiar with the workings of your home and estate and would manage them admirably."

What she meant was the girl had been living off his charity for years now, Wynn interpreted, and would continue to let Marissa rule the roost.

"She is a comfortable, conformable young woman who will not enact emotional scenes or interfere with your life in any way. She will ignore any, ah, little diversions in which you might indulge."

"Do you mean she would not mind if I keep a mistress or two?" Wynn asked. "She would be a docile little spouse, content with keeping my house, raising my children, spending my money?"

"Precisely. I knew you would see reason."

"I see a dismal future, madam. What makes you think I would want a wife who cared so little for me she would not mind sharing my affections or my bed?"

"Do not be vulgar, Ingall."

Wynn ignored her. "Well, I would want her to mind. In fact, I would want her to kick up a vulgar, emotional dust at the very thought of my keeping a mistress—the same as I would if my wife decided to take a lover. I would want her to have emotions and, yes, to take part in every aspect of my life, including my bed. I'll have no woman who does not welcome my lovemaking, nay, who is not eager for it."

Marissa's affronted gasp said much about her own marriage to Roger, the poor beggar.

Wynn concluded: "I refuse to countenance a marriage that is cold and merely courteous, no matter how convenient, no matter how respectable or *a la mode*."

Marissa squinted at him. "Heavens, I do believe you have given the matter some thought."

Hell, he must have.

*   *   *

The dinner was delicious.

Cousin Deanna was dutifully nondescript, her conversation dull.

And Wynn was dumbfounded. Could he really be considering . . . ? Was he truly contemplating . . . ?

Damn, he could not tie a proper neckcloth, much less that kind of knot.

Besides, he was still fodder for the gossips, still undecided about his future . . . and Lady Torrie still looked like a princess to him, sitting in a theater box not far from theirs. She had her hair piled atop her head, held with a gold fillet except for a few wispy curls that trailed down her neck, embracing her ears, caressing her cheeks, leading the eye to her soft, rosy, kissable lips. Lud, he thought, this was going to be another long night, and the play had not even started.

He was not to be granted the refuge of the drama onstage, either, for Marissa kept up a monologue of her own. She could barely see the actors, Wynn guessed, but the opera glasses that were commonplace here permitted her to scrutinize her fellow theatergoers without revealing her poor eyesight. Lady Phillips looked a quiz in an orange turban; Susanna Loft's escort was from a mere cadet branch of the Merrick clan; Sir Reginald was sharing his box with—

"Don't look in that direction, Deanna."

And on and on. Before the first intermission, Wynn had a précis of the pedigree of half the attendees, and a raging headache. Cousin Deanna looked worse.

"Are you feeling poorly?" he asked out of politeness, and a desire for an excuse to cut the evening short. Not that he had anything against the girl—except that he did not want her collapsing against him.

"I am just a trifle light-headed, my lord," she replied. "I shall be fine."

"Of course she will," Marissa said, as if her declaration could make it so. "The air is so stuffy in these boxes, it is a wonder everyone is not dizzy. Take her out in the corridor for some fresh air, Ingall, and fetch back some lemonade. No, you are paying. Make that champagne."

Wynn would have suspected a plot to throw him and Miss Herman together, except the girl truly did look ill, and she paced as far from him in the hallway as possible. When he would have taken her arm as the corridor became more crowded, she flinched away from him. Zeus, she wasn't afraid of him, too, was she?

"Marissa has not convinced you that I am a rake-shame, has she, Cousin Deanna?"

"Gracious, no." But she was clutching her shawl around her shoulders as if it were a shield.

"Have I offended you, then?"

She shook her head, biting her lip.

"You are not about to cast up your accounts, are you?"

She shook her head again.

Wynn looked around for the nearest exit, but all the stairwells and corridors were blocked with everyone else who sought to stretch their legs. He found a relatively empty space outside a vacant box and led her to it. "Then what is it? I cannot help if I do not know the problem."

She stared at her toes, pulling the shawl closer, and whispered, "I do not wish to marry you, my lord."

"That's all?" he asked with a laugh. "You must be the only unattached woman in London who does not."

"But Marissa says—"

"A great deal more than she ought. Now, smile, lest the tabbies accuse me of insulting your tender sensibilities. You may rest assured that I have no intention of asking you to be my wife, no matter what Marissa decrees. She does not control my destiny, as I take it she controls yours."

The girl accomplished a small smile, out of relief. "Oh, yes, I am completely dependent on her kindness."

"Which is all to her own purpose, I do not doubt. Tell me, is there a gentleman you do wish to wed that my suit would prove so burdensome?"

Now she blushed, but her lips turned up in a genuine smile at the thought of her beau. "Howard."

Wynn did not know any Howard, but he smiled back at how the chit went all starry-eyed at the mention of his name. She even began to look pretty. "Ah, Howard. I take it Howard does not find acceptance with my sister-in-law?"

The smile faded. "Howard is a mere curate, without a parish of his own. He cannot afford to take a wife, even if Marissa approved."

"But he wishes to wed? I mean, he does want to marry you?"

"Of course. Howard loves me as much as I love him."

Now there was a lucky fellow, Wynn thought, who knew what he wanted. A chosen vocation, a chosen woman. He simply had not yet attained any of his goals. Well, here was a nuptial problem that Wynn could resolve, finally. "I believe the Ingall viscountcy controls several livings. One or another is bound to be vacant because the churches are not in use, with the family never in residence. My man of affairs can look into it in the morning. We'll have your Howard a position before the month is out, and you can be a June bride."

"Truly? You'd do that, for me?"

"And to spite Marissa." They laughed together. "I'll even throw the wedding breakfast."

"My cousin is wrong. You really are a true gentleman. If not for Howard, I believe I would set my cap for you after all." She stood on tiptoe and quickly kissed his cheek.

Which was, of course, when Lady Victoria Keyes left her own box.

Torrie usually loved the theater, the spectacle, the excitement in the air, the noisy, cheerful crowds. Her aunt Ann hated everything about it except the action on the stage. She found the audience raucous and disrespectful, more interested in being seen themselves than seeing Mr. Shakespeare's enduring art. Why, she said, half of them thought Hamlet was a small pig. Still, she had come this evening as Torrie's companion. She would not, however, tolerate Torrie's lovesick swains littering the box during the drama, so she had the Duchamp footman, Henry, stand guard outside, refusing entry to all who asked.

At the interval, however, Aunt Ann sent Henry to run down the stairs to fetch them cooling drinks. Lord Boyce, who had been awaiting his chance, popped his head into the box before any other of Lady Torrie's suitors could reach it. He had a new plan, with the Scarecrow waiting outside the theater to carry it—and Lady Torrie—out. All he had to do was get the girl alone in the dark corridor for a minute. He could bash her on the head, claim she was ill, and have her down the stairs before the dragon of an aunt knew she was gone. He'd keep her, too, at the place the Scarecrow had found outside of London, until she agreed to marry him.

There were three problems with the plan: getting her to step outside the box with him, hitting her hard enough that she did not scream, and carrying her. Otherwise it was foolproof. He had chewed a hole in the knuckles of his evening gloves, waiting.

"Go walking in the hall with you, my lord?" Torrie asked, trying to keep her voice as low as possible and a polite smile on her face for those she knew were watching. "I do not think so. After your actions in the park, I am astounded you would ask."

"But you see, that is why you must come, so I can make a proper apology."

"Apologize for what?" Aunt Ann wanted to know, ready to do battle with Boyce.

Torrie did not want another scene. Neither did she want to lose sight of Wynn, who was leaving the Ingall family box with that cousin Lady Ingall was presenting this year. Torrie had been hoping he would pay a call on her and her aunt during the interval, but he had Miss Deanna Herman on his arm instead. Torrie thought perhaps she ought to go see how close the relationship was between those two, so she accepted Boyce's escort—and practically walked into the other couple, embracing. Good grief, they were kissing cousins! She spun on her heels and sailed back to her own box, leaving Lord Boyce in her wake.

"Come, Aunt Ann. We can leave. I have seen enough bad acting for one night."

Chapter Nineteen

"I cannot marry that man, Papa."

Lord Duchamp put down his newspaper and his pipe and sighed. "Of course not, my love. Ah, which man is that, that you will not wed this week? I only ask, you know, in case he seeks my permission first. Much less awkward for the poor chap."

"It is Viscount Ingall, of course. The man we have been discussing all week."

"Ah, that gentleman. I thought he had withdrawn himself from the lists of contenders. Was I wrong?"

Torrie brushed his query aside as if the viscount's wishes were of no account. "His name was at the top of the roster. Now it is not."

"Too bad. I quite liked the fellow. I thought you were determined to have him, too. Saved your life and all that." He went back to reading his paper.

"I am, of course, grateful for what he did, but Mama was right."

"She usually is," the earl murmured, only half listening. "Ah, what was she correct about this time?"

"That one should not select a husband by the turn of a card."

Lord Duchamp put the paper down again. "Of course your mother was right. Only a pea-goose would gamble on picking a winner out of a deck of pasteboards. You are speaking of a husband, not a magic trick."

"I know, Papa, and I swear I would not simply choose a name out of a hat. But Mama meant I should not put my trust in luck to find the perfect husband. That I had to get to know the man, to determine his character, to build an understanding, a foundation for a lasting, loving relationship."

"Wise woman, your mother. Except when she gets a bee in her bonnet about taking off for York in the middle of the Season. I have to admit I was hoping you'd settled on Ingall and we could go home as soon as you brought him up to scratch."

"I know, Papa, but Lord Ingall simply will not suit. His moral fiber does not bear scrutiny."

"You haven't been listening to six-year-old gossip, have you? I told you, everything about that duel is better forgotten."

It would have been better if the viscount had forgotten it, too, and the women he fought it over. He had not, and Torrie could not. "No, Papa, I am not speaking of his past conduct, but of his current liaisons."

"What, listening to the rumor mills? You know how the chaw-bacons like to shred a man's character just for the fun of it, especially a well setup, manly chap."

"This is not idle rumor. I saw the man myself with three different women, in various states of shocking public behavior."

"Three, by George? Not at once, I hope. I mean, are you certain you saw three?"

"I am positive. One in the park, one at the dressmakers, and one at the theater. Who knows how many other women he fondles." Torrie was outraged anew that he had added her name to a long list. She was outraged, dismayed, and so disappointed she could cry—and had all night. Her hero was a hedonist, not husband material. He might be damned to hell, but so was she, for caring.

"Fondles, eh? In public?"

She nodded. "I saw them with my own eyes, women

from all walks of life. Who knows what he promises them, wardrobes from Madame Michaela or wedding bells? I would not take his word for tuppence."

"By Zeus, you cannot marry the libertine, Torrie. I refuse to give my permission and that is final. I never did hold much stock in sacred vows and that fustian."

Torrie swallowed past a lump in her throat, knowing she was letting both of them down. "Of course you did, Papa. You always taught me that the definition of an honorable man was one whose word could be trusted."

Now her father appeared uncomfortable. He straightened the already neat edges of his newspaper. "Yes, but I was speaking of bargains between gentlemen, deals signed with handshakes and all that."

"Is a woman less dishonorable for breaking her promises?"

Lord Duchamp had no answer, so he asked one back: "But you never promised Ingall that you would marry him, did you?"

Torrie had sworn to marry the man who saved her, but she had not made that vow to Wynn, just a request. Which he had refused, thank goodness. "No, and I doubt his lordship would be trying to sue for breach of promise anyway." He seemed to have no interest in marrying at all, unless he could have a harem.

"That's all right and tight, then."

"No, it is not, Papa. I said I would marry and I shall. I am determined on keeping that much of my oath, of my honor. The bridegroom will be different, that is all. I shall go to Mrs. Reese's ball, where every eligible gentleman of the *ton* will be gathered, and I will select one there. I know them all, their bad habits and their bank accounts, so it will not be a matter of buying a pig in a poke."

"But you have turned them all down in the past."

"I am no longer so particular. I foolishly used to expect the ground to tremble when the man of my dreams approached. Now I realize I was waiting for an earthquake, not a living, breathing husband. Do not worry, Papa, I shall pick one whom we both can respect, and hope that love will follow."

"Are you certain, poppet? I would not wish you to choose a man just so we can join your mother that much sooner."

"I am certain. Aside from my vow, it is long past time I wed and began a life of my own, a nursery of my own." Whose inhabitants would not have moss-green eyes, to her sorrow. She touched the diamond key at her neck, then lowered her hand quickly.

"Pray for sons, poppet. They won't make you old before your time the way you are doing to me."

"What fustian. You are still in your prime. Why, I will wager that all the ladies at Mrs. Reese's ball will be lined up for a dance with you, what with Mama not there."

"Mrs. Reese's ball?" His mouth dropped open.

"Of course. Since I am not going to marry Lord Ingall, I do not wish his escort. You will have to go with me."

"Me? Devil a bit. You can take Henry and five other footmen."

"But you must be handy to give your blessings and announce the betrothal so it is official." And so Torrie could not back out after making her selection, but she did not say that.

Lord Duchamp put his head in his hands, muttering something else about daughters, serpent's teeth, and plagues. Torrie did not see what he had to complain of. After all, she was going to be the one having to pick a man who was less heroic than Lord Ingall. Less of a self-assured, self-made man than Lord Ingall. Less exciting and entrancing than Lord Ingall. Worst of all, after she picked him, she was going to have to marry the man who was anyone except Lord Ingall.

"I regret, my lord," the Keyes butler intoned, "that the ladies are not at home."

Wynn knew they were in. He still had Barrogi and the

new man watching the house. He fished a coin from his pocket. "Mallen, is it? I do believe we have danced this measure before."

Mallen looked at the coin, and at the openhanded, genuinely gentlemanly gentleman, and shook his silvered head with regret.

"What, is Lady Torrie not feeling well? Occupied with a suitor? Still at her bath?" Wynn would wait. Now that he decided to call, he was not leaving until he had said his piece.

The poor, loyal butler could only shake his head again. He had his orders.

"I . . . understand." It was Wynn she was not home to.

Homer did not understand. He darted between Mallen's legs and down the hall, barking outside the morning room until the door opened.

Torrie looked out. "Oh, Lord Ingall. I was just penning you a letter."

"You may save yourself the effort. I am here, as you can see."

She saw the last person on earth she wished to, despite her best efforts to keep him out of her house and her thoughts. Mallen was nodding approvingly. Torrie wished him to perdition, along with all old, interfering family retainers who thought they knew better than their employers. "I suppose you had ought to come in, then, my lord."

This was not precisely the welcome Wynn had envisioned when he planned this morning call, but he followed Homer into the room.

"I shall bring tea," Mallen said before departing. He left the door slightly open behind him, as was proper, if not up to the letter of punctilio, with the aunt not present.

Torrie was looking like a bouquet in sprigged muslin, Wynn thought as he took the chair she indicated, across from a small writing table. All sunshine and flowers, she even smelled like spring. She stoppered the bottle of ink, straightened the sheets of paper, bent to pet the dog, then fiddled with the gold and diamond charm at her neck. Why, she was as nervous as he was, Wynn realized, trying to drag his eyes from where the charm lay against her creamy skin. How could she be, when she did not know why he had come?

"Lady Torrie—" he began at the same time she said, "Lord Ingall, I—"

"You go first."

"No, you."

"Very well." Wynn cleared his throat. "I, ah, I have come for three reasons. The first is to explain about last night, since you left before I could make you known to Miss Herman."

"No explanation is necessary, my lord. Whatever you choose to do in the halls of the theater is your concern, not mine."

There, Wynn told himself, she did trust him! Excellent. "My second reason for calling is to ask what time to fetch you and your aunt for Mrs. Reese's ball."

Torrie firmed her spine. If she straightened any more, she would break. "My lord, as I was trying to convey in my letter, I would not attend a funeral with you, unless it was yours, much less a ball. I never wish to see such a disreputable, dishonorable dastard again. Nor would Mrs. Reese, if she knew your true colors. Now, what was your third reason for calling, before you leave?"

"To ask you to marry me."

"What?" she nearly screamed, catching herself in time just as Mallen entered the room with a heavy tray. She silently made space on the table and rearranged the plates and cups until the old man left. Then it was not tea she poured out. "Why, you, you cad! I would not marry you if you were the last man in creation! I heard you promise Miss Herman a wedding, and I heard you promise Lady Lynbrook a new wardrobe. I was in the back of Madame Michaela's shop, having a fitting. Heaven only knows what you promised that poor girl who is enceinte, you, fork-tongued devil, you, before you started pawing at me."

"Why, you are jealous."

"Jealous? Of a wandering-eyed, womanizing worm? Hah! As if I would wed a poltroon who cannot restrain his base desires! Isn't that just like a man, though. You behave like the village tom, then accuse me of being cattish. Get out, you and your pesky dog, too." She threw a biscuit toward the door to get Homer, at least, to head in that direction.

Wynn started to follow, but then stopped, not that he was begging for crumbs, of course. "What about Fate, about our being meant for each other?"

"You said you do not believe in that tripe."

"What about your vow?"

She threw the next biscuit at his head.

Crushed. Wadded into a small ball and thrown to the ground, then kicked. That was his neckcloth. Wynn's feelings were suffering worse.

Blasted female. Blast all females. The world would be a better place without them. Emptier, but better. At least a fellow would know where he stood. Here he had spent the whole night thinking about marriage, about how it might not be the worst thing in the world after being drawn and quartered. In fact, he'd come to the conclusion that he would be better off wed to Lady Torrie than alone, prey to every marriageable miss and her mama. He did not care about the succession, but a child of his own might not be a bad idea, especially a child with Torrie's red-gold curls and blue eyes. He had not been able to think of anything but her and her eyes—and her lips and her smile and the feel of her in his arms—since he'd carried her from that fire, so why not marry her? The earl's daughter was not in need of his money, had already accepted his past—and was guaranteed to accept his formal offer. She'd asked him, by Jupiter!

Women! Bah! He'd take a good, loyal dog any day. Of course, he'd had to take Homer by the collar and drag him from Duchamp House, with its airborne edibles.

Chapter Twenty

"Wish me happy, Papa." Torrie was interrupting her father for yet another time. "I have rid myself of that despicable man for well and good."

"Um, which one was that, again?"

"Viscount Ingall, of course. I made sure the libertine knew he would not be welcome to call here. Good riddance, I say."

The earl looked at her over his newspaper. "If you are so pleased with yourself, poppet, why are you crying?"

"Crying? I am doing no such thing," she said with a sniffle. "The cad brought that silly dog of his. The mongrel's fur must have irritated my eyes, that's all."

Lord Duchamp thought about all the hounds and horses and barn cats at Dubron, none of which had ever bothered his daughter before. "Your mama always bathed her eyes with a cloth soaked in lavender water when she'd been weep— that is, when she was so afflicted. You might consider doing that, if you were going to go to the park or out visiting this afternoon. You wouldn't want the gossips saying you'd been cry— that is, that you are a sickly puss."

"Thank you, Papa. I do not think I will be going out today, however. It looks like rain."

The day was gray, like most days in London. That had never stopped Torrie from gadding all about town, either. "Yes, you want to save your strength for the Reese ball, eh? I daresay you'll need it, if you are still determined to find yourself a husband there."

"Of course I am. I told you so this morning." Why not? Torrie was afraid she would never find a man who so stirred her senses, who so stirred her heart, as Viscount Ingall. Since her hero had feet of clay, she might as well settle for the least obnoxious of her suitors. "Nothing has changed since." Except her shattered hopes.

"Then heaven help you, my dear." And heaven help him, Lord Duchamp prayed, when his wife got wind of their daughter's latest start.

Wynn snapped his fingers. He could find a woman to wed as quickly as that, he told himself. Then he had to scratch behind Homer's ears, for the dumb dog thought he was being called for a walk or a snack.

Why, he was rich and wellborn, and since Boyce's best efforts had been countered by Lord Duchamp's and Marissa's, he was accepted most places except Almack's, where he never wished to go, and now Duchamp House. The earl had put his name up at White's and seen that he was voted in, so Wynn was now a member of that august body. In some addled way, the *ton* had decided that members of the gentlemen's club must therefore be gentlemen, placing him once more on the invitations lists. Or perhaps his fortune had outweighed his reputation. Or his bachelorhood had. Most of the cards on his mantel were to come-out parties or amateur musicales where the young women could show off their talents, as if harp-playing were requisite in a wife.

No, Wynn thought, he would have no problem finding an accomplished, accommodating wife now that he had decided he needed one. Lady Torrie, on the other hand, with her finicky, supercilious air of superiority and her haste to find all men wanting, could end her days leading apes in hell.

Somehow the notion did not please him as much as he'd thought it would. Nor did the idea of attending any of those dances or come-out balls. Now he had a choice, though. Now he could go to his club and get drunk and gamble his fortune away, which was the age-old remedy for a broken heart. Not that his was broken, of course. Just slightly bruised. Actually, he told himself, it was more his self-esteem that had been battered, his pride beaten to a pulp. He did not give that—another snap of his fingers; another miscue to the cur—for Lady Victoria Ann Keyes. No, he would visit White's and pick a likely husband for Bette, Lady Lynbrook. Making another man miserable was a much better way of spending his evening.

First, he had to dress. For once he was confident of being turned out in proper fashion, as Marissa had kept her word and sent Redding to him. His brother's former valet was a perfectionist, a boot-polishing paragon, and a prig. Just what Wynn needed.

He was a tall, well-built man, close to Wynn in age, with carefully smoothed blond locks and high cheekbones.

"At least this one, he is pretty," Barrogi commented as they waited for Redding to evaluate his new employer's wardrobe, physique, and circumstances.

Redding rocked on his heels, flared his nostrils, and spoke. He enunciated each word so carefully, the sibilants sprayed across the small space.

"Where I *ss*erve there are no dog*ss*." He curled his lip at Barrogi. "No foreigner*ss*. No 'pretty' fellow*ss*."

No valet.

Before Barrogi could boot the swine down the front steps, Wynn asked how long he had been on the Ingram House payroll.

"For the previous six years, my lord."

"Although my brother has been dead for the last two of them?"

Redding rocked back and forth. "That is correct. I have been acting as assistant to Lady Ingall."

Marissa was so busy managing other people's lives that she needed a personal secretary? A handsome, strapping fellow? "Exactly what is it that you do for my sister-in-law, if you do not mind my asking? I feel entitled to inquire, you see, since I am the one who actually pays your salary."

Redding rocked some more, not replying.

"You write her correspondence and keep her social calendar?"

Redding nodded. "Precisely."

Wynn wiped his cheek.

"And you run her errands and escort her on calls?"

"When required. I also advise madam about fashions, plan her journeys, and balance her accounts."

Which would take about an hour a day. What did the man do with his nights, Wynn asked. Redding did not answer, which was answer enough.

"You warm her bed?"

"I . . . I . . ."

"You are a braver man than I, Redding. Ssoldier on."

Wynn was delighted with that turn of events, despite finding himself sans valet. Now he had a bargaining tool for dealing with Marissa, who had yet to give Deanna and Howard her blessing. He would not exactly call it blackmail, for he would never reveal the *ton* that the very proper Lady Ingall enjoyed a very close propinquity with her dead husband's valet—but Marissa did not have to know that. When he went to report that he had made arrangements for Deanna's cleric to have a living at St. Abner's near Caswell, he also asked Marissa a favor. Would she please invite Bette to a few of her afternoon at-homes, an evening of cards, or to share her box—Wynn's family box—at the opera?

Marissa peered at him as if he'd sprouted antlers. "First you convince my cousin to throw her life away in a moldering manse, and now you are asking me to entertain Lynbrook's light skirt?"

"No, the light skirt was Rosie. Bette is his respectable

widow. If you have her at Ingram House, the ladies will see she is neither fast nor a social misfit."

"Never."

Wynn merely had to say "I *ssee*," with a cock-of-the-walk smile on his face.

"I suppose I could invite her for tea one afternoon."

Wynn rocked on the balls of his feet a time or two, touched the lumpish linen at his throat, and raised his eyebrow.

"Oh, very well. A small dinner or something."

Wynn decided that one good turn deserved another. If Marissa made Bette acceptable, he would see about making Redding a shade more respectable.

Mrs. Reese was easier, if no less underhanded. Wynn had only to bribe her with a roof for her charity school to secure Bette an invitation to the ball. As the little old lady was writing out the card, however, she paused with her pen in the air. "You know, the school will not do the children much good if they are too hungry to study. If they go to work, or start stealing in order to put food in their bellies, they cannot have time for their lessons."

So he promised to finance the kitchen, too, and keep it stocked.

She sanded the invitation and waved it, out of reach, while it dried. So he became a benefactor to a hospital, where the children might get care.

She might look like an ancient gnome, Wynn decided, but Mrs. Reese had the fortitude of an elephant and the wiles of a fox. Born to a titled family, she had married well, but well beneath her. Now her Croesus of a coal merchant was six feet beneath the ground, and the widow had bought her way back into the *ton*. Her invitations were highly sought after, her approval almost necessary for a young girl's successful come-out. And she wanted a pound of flesh for her favor.

Wynn had the invitation when he left.

He had a great deal less money than when he arrived.

And he had a position as trustee of the school, the hospital, and an orphanage that got added while he was putting the card in his pocket. A fellow could do worse, Wynn decided, than use his time and money and skills to improve the lives of those less fortunate. He'd make more of a difference this way, too, than sitting in Parliament with the pettifogging politicians. And he could still learn to oversee his estates and raise prime cattle if he wanted.

Yes, Wynn decided, his future was looking rosier. But first he had to find a husband for Rosie.

He had made a good start to putting Bette in the way of eligible gentlemen, and better by letting it be known in the gentlemen's clubs that she was not entirely penniless. Wynn could not begin to think, however, where to look for a father for a Paphian's progeny, no matter how much brass he had to provide.

Rosie was not as despondent as she had been, thank goodness, nor as weepy. Perhaps she was happier because she was not alone all the time, or perhaps it was because she was respected in her neighborhood now. When one of the local boys had called out an insult, Barrogi had sharpened his knife. Rosie was treated like a lady after that.

"Don't worry, love," she told Wynn. "I'm sure you'll think of something sooner or later."

Her confidence in him was heartening, but time was running out for the baby—and for finding a valet to get him ready for Mrs. Reese's ball.

Wynn was disgusted with the offerings of the Day brothers' agency. They had recently sent him three valets: one man was so efficient he awakened Wynn with a booming voice that rattled the windows, before dawn; another was so efficient he tried to groom the dog, who took exception to the scissors, the comb, and the clunch; the third man was so efficient he kept sampling Wynn's wine, to make sure it was not poisoned. Then the agency sent a note that they were closing their doors.

A man who had made his own way around the world had to be able to tie his own neckcloth, Wynn insisted to himself. Besides, he was desperate. So he went to Rosie for lessons. First she showed him how on Barrogi, who blushed, the old dog. Then she had Wynn practice on Barrogi, who growled, worse than the clean-shaven dog. Then Wynn got to tie his own in front of her hazy pier glass. He tied them and tied them, enough for Mrs. Reese's whole school of boys to look like unhappy little gentlemen. His neck was chafed, his fingers were numb, his eyes were all but crossed, but he could manage a perfect fold at least most of the time.

He spent most of the afternoon before the ball getting ready, feeling like a girl preparing for her first grown-up party. Everything had to be perfect. He could not appear gauche to his sister-in-law, whom he was escorting, nor raffish, lest he rake up the old scandal about Bette, who was also in their party. Getting Marissa to take Bette up in her carriage had taken almost as long as tying the perfect Windfall. If it wasn't Wynn's carriage, in fact, he doubted the outcome, Redding or no Redding. Most of all, his appearance had to be top of the trees, to show a certain featherheaded female that he was not entirely beneath contempt, that other women found him attractive.

Three hours later, Wynn was ready for battle, and ready to face Lady Torrie. That is, he was ready to find a lady of his own.

If clothes made the man, he would have a fiancée by morning. If clothes did not, he could fall back on his title and fortune.

Marissa came with her cousin in the town carriage to fetch him, right on time, of course. Wynn dutifully complimented both ladies on their ensembles, although all he could see by the dim couch lamps were dark capes and the Ingall diamonds gleaming magnificently around his sister-in-law's greedy throat.

When they arrived at Lynbrook House, Wynn went

in to collect Bette. She was not ready, naturally. While he waited, Wynn adjusted his lace cuffs, made sure the chain to his fob watch had not become entangled in his waistcoat buttons, and checked to see that his beard had not grown in the three hours since he'd shaved—and all without turning his head, lest he ruin the masterpiece at his throat.

Then Bette skipped down the hall in her shepherdess costume, crook and all.

Chapter Twenty-one

"It's a bloody masquerade?"

"Of course it is. Everyone knows Mrs. Reese's annual costume ball is the highlight of the social Season. I suppose you left your mask in the carriage, although I thought you could do better than evening dress and a domino."

He could do a great deal better. He could pretend to be a berserker, strangling Bette, his sister-in-law, and Madame Michaela, any one of whom could have told him the party was a blasted masquerade. The female he blamed most of all, of course, was Lady Torrie, for getting him started on this path in the first place. He would not have to pretend to be a Bedlamite, if he had his hands at her conniving, contrary, confounded neck.

Bette twirled her feathered mask, showing lace petticoats and red stockings no shepherdess could afford. Neither could Bette. Wynn had paid for the cursed costume, to boot. Botheration!

He nearly shoved Bette into the carriage with the others, saying he would join them later, that they would be less recognizable without his escort. Hah! By the added lights of Lynbrook House, Wynn could now see that Marissa was in her habitual black, this time striped with white. He doubted more than a handful of the guests had ever seen a zebra, unless there was one in the royal menagerie, so her costume was accidental. Prim and proper Deanna was demure in a nun's habit. He had no doubt her Howard would be a monk. How original. As for Bette, no one who had ever met her could mistake that giggle, or the jiggle of her ample endowments in that low, ribbon-tied blouse.

A masquerade, by George. He'd wasted his entire day getting prettified for a demmed costume party. The only thing Wynn liked less than waltzing around in all his finery was acting the jester in motley. What was wrong with these people that they had nothing better to do with their lives than play at children's games? Is this why he had worked so hard to come back to England?

He had already pulled the wretched neckcloth off, along with his swallow-tailed coat and pinstriped waistcoat, before the hackney driver pulled to a stop outside his Kensington residence. He ripped off the white satin knee breeches as soon as he got in the door.

"Fleas, eh?" Barrogi gestured toward the dog. "I told you how it would be."

"Not bugs. A blasted masquerade."

"I thought you knew that, *padrone*. You were pretending to be a lovesick swine, no?"

"A swain and, no, I was not! I am not. I was dressing like a deuced English lordling, which I am, dash it."

Wynn pulled open the collar of his shirt and tied one of Barrogi's clean red kerchiefs around his neck. He found his oldest buckskins and his favorite soft, scuffed boots. Then he dragged a paisley cloth off one of the side tables, rolled it, and belted it around his waist, letting the fringed ends hang down. He stuck a jeweled but serviceable dagger, in its sheath, into the sash. No hat, no gloves, no ruby tie pin.

"No mask, *padrone*? You could borrow mine."

Wynn did not want to consider why Barrogi had a mask. "No. It is about time these apathetic excuses for aristocrats saw the real Wynn Ingram. No more costumes, no more masks. If they don't like it, they can go hang."

*   *   *

"We're gonna hang for this, you daft old dandy."

"Shut up and put on the mask. No one will notice us in the crowd."

"What am I supposed to be, then?"

Boyce glared at his henchman by the light of the shielded lantern. "You are supposed to be watching for an opening in this blasted hedge so we do not have to climb the side walls to get into the damned garden. What you look like is a grave robber."

"That's all right then. Pays better'n a grave digger. Speakin' of which, I ain't gettin' paid to crawl around in the dirt behind some gentry mort's mansion. In fact, I ain't gettin' paid at all, that I can notice."

"Stubble it. I told you you'd get paid as soon as we get the girl. It'll be better this way." This way the Scarecrow could be the one to hit Lady Torrie over the head and carry her to the wagon they had waiting around the block, behind the stable mews. All Lord Boyce had to do was entice her out to the gardens and down one of the ill-lit paths. Then they'd have her all right and tight, stuffed in a big sack Scarecrow had tucked in his breeches. The plan was for Boyce to play the hero, rescuing her. If she failed to be suitably grateful, they'd keep going to that abandoned cottage. If she still would not marry him after being thoroughly compromised, Boyce planned on getting a handsome ransom from her father. He'd have to sail away, of course, but the cents-per-centers he owed were going to send him on an ocean journey anyway—without the ship.

"She ain't never gonna go off with you, not after last time."

"She will if she does not recognize me." Boyce was dressed as a knight of old in a chain mail doublet, complete with visored helmet and a lance with which he was prodding the yew hedges.

"How're you gonna recognize the chit, then, if everyone's in costume?"

That was the easy part. Lady Torrie would be the woman with all the other fortune hunters at her feet.

Names were not being announced at the entrance, of course, this being a masquerade, yet Torrie and her father paused at the top of the stairway leading down to the ballroom. Since she would be coming on her father's arm, with her aunt as chaperon, and both of them had refused to don so much as a half mask, Torrie had not hidden her face either. She even wore her well-known gold and diamond key. After all, she wanted her chosen gentleman to propose to her, not to an unknown nymph or gypsy. This was not the time for flirting with gentlemen she could not recognize, either. The time for hidden glances and secret smiles, the shiver of wondering if this man was the one, if that mask hid the face she would come to love—that thrill of anticipation was long gone, never to return.

"Smile, poppet, your court awaits."

The crowds below caught sight of the new arrivals, and nearly a score of cavaliers, Romans, and Robin Hoods surged in their direction. "Like racehorses to the starting gate," Aunt Ann murmured from Torrie's other side.

"At least they are all Thoroughbreds. Louisa Reese wouldn't have anything less," the earl said, frowning at his sister. Then he turned to Torrie. "It's your field, my dear. Pick us a winner."

All Torrie saw was a field of broken dreams, but she pasted a smile on her face and prepared to meet her destiny.

In almost no time at all, she had sorted out the gentlemen clamoring for her attention. Sir Eric, Lord Mayfield, and Baron Knowles had been three of her most stalwart suitors for years. Any one of them would make an adequate, if uninspiring spouse. She granted them each a dance.

"I'll be in the card room if you need me," Lord Du-champ said loudly enough to be heard by the gentlemen, one of whom he was hoping would seek him out before supper, so they could go home after the lobster patties.

Aunt Ann took up her vantage point in the row of gilt chairs along the dance floor's edges. She took out her needlework. If her niece did not know her way around a ballroom by now, it was far too late for a maiden aunt to teach her.

Her father was gone, her aunt was gone, and Torrie was alone to make the decision of her life.

Sir Eric was one of the most handsome men in London, with perfect manners and elegant dress. He was a superb dancer and a charming conversationalist. Everything Lord Ingall was not, in fact. The baronet even had an adequate income. He made a more than adequate Greek god in his short toga and leather sandals. Best of all, he had proposed to Torrie in the past. How hard could it be to coax another offer from him tonight?

As hard as one of the fluted columns that held up the ceiling of the ballroom. While Torrie and Sir Eric walked to the dance floor, his eyes swiveled toward a giggling shepherdess who was showing more of her ankles than was proper—and more of her bosom than was polite, more than Torrie had dared, in fact. Torrie recognized that giggle as belonging to the woman at Madame Michaela's, the woman who belonged to Lord In-gall, although the Cossack at her side was much too short and squat to be the viscount. Knowing Wynn had to be somewhere in the vicinity, she looked around for him, wondering what costume he would choose and if she would recognize the cad in ample time to ignore him. Sir Eric looked around, too, at the round, swaying posterior of Lady Lynbrook, and walked smack into the column.

Now Sir Eric was not quite so handsome, with a huge goose-egg forming on his temple. His toga was not so elegant with blood dripping down it, either. Two footmen with towels had to come lead him away while three women fluttered in his wake. Torrie did not stay in the anteroom with them, seeing that the baronet would have sufficient care. She did not care to be a member of his entourage. She'd had a lucky escape, it seemed. Although not so lucky for Sir Eric, the disaster had shown his true colors. The man could never be content with one woman, and Torrie could not accept that. Why, if she wanted a womanizer to wed, she could have had Wynn, who did not walk into the architecture.

By the time she got back to the ballroom, Torrie had missed half her quadrille with Lord Knowles, which was no bad thing. The baron was one of the clumsiest dancers she knew, but he was sweet-natured and kind to his mother. A woman was not supposed to dance too often with her own husband at any rate, and a pleasant disposition was far more important than a nimble foot . . . or a full head of hair . . . or even teeth. That is what she told herself, anyway.

Rather than try to join the ongoing dance, they decided to stroll about the ballroom periphery—Torrie in her gold costume, Lord Knowles in an embroidered silver tunic. He was supposed to represent Sir Galahad, she thought, but he kept tripping over the sword at his side.

He led her toward where his mother sat and Torrie politely inquired into the older woman's health, not expecting an actual recounting of every ache and pain the woman had suffered since the turn of the century. Torrie took the opportunity to survey the dancers. The Lynbrook woman was dancing with a different man now, a minstrel who was far too spindly-legged for his hose, much less for Lord Ingall, but she was still giggling. At least someone was having a good time.

Lady Knowles finally wound down, telling her son she was dying of thirst. "Go fetch me a drink, Joseph, and none of that orgeat, mind. I want wine."

It was no wonder the old woman was parched. But when they reached the refreshments room, Lord

Knowles slipped on a wet patch, pitched into the table, and spilled all the punch. His shoes went flying in one direction, his hairpiece in another.

It took four footmen this time, for two of them had to carry Lord Knowles's mother out, too.

Well, perhaps the baron was a trifle too attached to his mother, Torrie thought. A mature man, a husband, for instance, ought not cry out for his mama in moments of stress. A good thing she had seen that—and his bald pate—before it was too late.

On her way to join her aunt before the next set, Torrie noticed Lady Ingall's cousin dancing. Heavens, were all of the viscount's paramours present tonight? Miss Herman's partner was a fair-haired friar, though, not the viscount. Deanna seemed delighted anyway. Ingall must be losing his touch, Torrie thought as she sought her own next partner.

Lord Mayfield was another nice gentleman, if somewhat shy. At least he would not be getting up flirtations with every woman he met. Torrie was running out of time—and choices—so she asked if they could stroll on the terrace, instead of taking part in the contra-danse now forming. "Oh, I say. . . . That is, I am not sure . . ."

She took his arm. "My aunt won't mind, and it is a bit stuffy in here."

So they went through the open doors to the terrace, where Torrie led her prey—her *parti*—to the farthest corner, away from the ballroom lights.

"Oh, I say . . . the dark."

"Is so romantic, don't you think?" Torrie hinted.

There was enough light for her to see his Adam's apple bob as Mayfield gulped. "I . . . I say we had not ought . . . That is, oh dear."

Was the man a complete slowtop? Torrie could not very well propose to him, could she? No, she'd done that once, with disastrous results. She stepped closer.

"Oh, my." He stepped back.

Torrie took another step toward him. "Yes? Is there something you want to say to me?"

He took another step back. "I . . . I . . ."

Torrie pictured endless dinners waiting for him to ask her to pass the salt. Still, she persevered. "Something of a particular nature?" She moved close enough to lay her hand on his chest.

"I say . . ."

She would never know what the clunch was going to say because he took one more step backward, away from her, and tumbled down the terrace steps.

Chapter Twenty-two

The footmen were looking at Torrie oddly. One man crossed himself. Even she had to admit there had been an inordinate amount of bad luck this evening, almost as if the Fates were conspiring to keep her from marrying any man but— No, that was absurd. She simply had to try harder, that was all.

Torrie went to the ladies' retiring room to fix her hair. Ruthie had been out of sorts again tonight, so it was not pinned as securely as usual. Then again, the night had proved more strenuous than expected. She really had to see about Ruthie's health in the morning, for she liked the woman, in addition to needing her. Ruthie would have to wait for tomorrow. Tonight Torrie had to find a husband.

When she returned to the ballroom, she surveyed the remaining bachelors. Mr. Gilmartin was dressed as Bottom. Torrie refused to marry any man who resembled either end of an ass. Sir Jason swept her a courtly bow, and knocked over a servant's tray of wineglasses with his out-flung arm. She was not exactly sure of the identity of the Pierrot who asked her for the next dance, but she was sure he had not bathed in weeks.

Then she saw him. He was bent over to kiss Mrs. Reese's wrinkled cheek. Heavens, was no woman safe from Ingall's blandishments? He was dressed as a corsair, she thought, strong, bold, and dangerous. With his proud nose and wide stance, to say nothing of his trim waist, bright smile, and shining brown locks, he was the answer to every maiden's prayers—if she had been praying to be the heroine of a novel. Torrie had no intention of being the latest victim of his lordship's seductive spell, so she turned her back to find her next partner. With any luck, he'd turn into her life's partner, whomever he was.

Wynn greeted his hostess, then looked around to make sure the females he was supposed to be escorting had arrived safely. Marissa had found a high-backed chair from which to hold court. Cousin Deanna was radiant in the arms of a cowled monk. Bette was looking years younger as she bounced from partner to partner down the line of the dance. Surely one of the preening peacocks would claim her as a prize.

Then he saw her. Like him, Lady Torrie wore no mask, but she had a coronet of gold leaves woven through her curls. She was wearing a thoroughly inadequate amount of some clinging gold fabric, loosely draped in the semblance of a Greek chiton, with the crisscrossing bodice leaving one breast barely covered, and the other half exposed.

Wynn could not swallow, and he was not even wearing a tight neckcloth. His mouth was dry, his pulse was racing, and he had to pull the dangling ends of his tablecloth sash around to the front of his breeches. Then she turned and he could see a tiny pair of gold gossamer wings affixed to the back of her gown. Nike, of course. Winged Victory. One inch less fabric and she would have been Wanton Victory, with her gold sandals and painted toenails.

No, he thought, she should have been Diana, with her bow and arrows, for Lady Victoria was obviously on the hunt. He saw her reject one prospective dance partner after the other, as if no man could meet her impossible standards. She looked in his direction, raised her chin, and walked away.

Well, whatever game Winged Victory was playing, Wynn vowed, she would not win. He'd find himself a more beautiful, more charming, more passionate wife than she could ever have been. In his dreams. In London, he would settle for a girl with a good heart.

He did not have much better luck than Torrie.

The first young lady Mrs. Reese introduced him to fainted. He carried her to an anteroom that was, oddly enough, already employed as a field hospital. English balls must have changed more than he'd thought, that they kept a surgeon on hand.

The next female, he judged, pretended a swoon so he might carry her, too. Mrs. Reese splashed the contents of her wineglass in the chit's face, to put an end to that nonsense, as she put it.

The third young lady got some of her seven veils twisted in the knife hilt at his waist. When he pulled the dagger to free her, the diaphanous stuff ripped, leaving her two veils short of modesty, with her petticoat showing.

Perhaps this was not going to be the easy victory Wynn thought.

Mrs. Reese, bent on matchmaking for her favorite benefactor, thought he ought to dance, to meet all the females in a given set, but Wynn had been out of the habit for too long to remember half the steps of the line dances. He'd never liked the posturing, toe-pointing minuet, and the quadrille was for ballet dancers, he considered, not men in boots. Which left the waltz, but unfortunately carried overtones he was not yet ready to have heard by an unknown female. So he decided to ask Bette, to see how she was faring, and if she had met any likely candidates. It was late enough in the evening, and she had danced with enough other gentlemen, that no one could cry foul at one waltz between old friends.

She was too short for him, though, and he had to bend

his neck to listen to her excited chatter, so they decided to sit the dance out, on the sidelines.

Torrie looked over—it seemed she always knew where Viscount Ingall was, as if his presence drew her glance like a magnet—to see Lady Lynbrook draped across him as close as a neckcloth, if he were wearing one. Torrie turned and accepted the arm of the first gentleman who offered. He was a knight, who declared that even his light armor was devilishly warm, so could they take a turn in the garden?

With his voice muffled through his visor, Torrie did not know who the knight was, nor why the gudgeon did not remove his helmet if he was hot. She nodded to his suggestion, however, rather than watch Lord Ingall make a cake of himself over the dumpling-like dowager Lady Lynbrook. She and her Sir Stifling went back to the terrace, so she missed the incident in the ballroom.

Wynn and Bette were having a comfortable coze in the gilt chairs. She had not danced so much in years, Bette told him, nor had so many compliments. Unfortunately, she confessed, Bette now found herself out of breath, her feet aching, her head spinning.

"Oh, Wynn," she complained, "I am too old for this."

"You are not going to start crying again, are you?" Lud, they were both being treated as equals here, not outcasts. One of Bette's scenes could do just what Wynn wanted to avoid: still up the old scandal. Besides, no man wanted to wed a watering pot. He'd never get Bette fired off if the eligibles thought she was weepy, or still entangled with him.

Luckily, a commotion at the top of the stairs diverted her attention. A hush fell over the entire room, and all eyes turned to the late arrivals. Wellington himself stood there, the Iron Duke. This was better for the success of Mrs. Reese's party than an appearance by the prince or the tsar. It was almost as good as an appearance of one of the archangels. The tiny old lady scurried up the stairs, chiding her butler to announce their honored guest, even though no other names had been called that evening.

"Nonsense," the hero of the Peninsula countermanded in a voice that could be heard across battlefields, much less a London ballroom. "Everyone knows who I am anyway. But announce my young friend's name. He's the real guest of honor."

Behind the general, the watchers now saw, was a ribbon- and medallion-strewn officer in a wheeled Bath chair. His face was as scarlet as his coat, as two burly soldiers started to lift the chair to carry it down the stairs. He must have demurred, for his commander slapped him on the back. "Bosh. You said you had friends here, and that's the only way you can find them, Major Campe."

"Troy?" Bette screamed before collapsing into Wynn's arms. He felt like fainting himself. It truly was his friend Troy, returned from the dead, or from whatever hell the war had taken him. He was not going to wait for those blasted soldiers to bump Troy down the steps. He bounded up them instead, with Bette hanging limp in his embrace. He dumped her into Troy's lap, saying, "I think this belongs to you," then fell to his knees to wrap his arms around his oldest best friend.

"I see your friends found you after all," Wellington said, wiping a tear from his own eye before signaling the soldiers to stand away. "Ingall, is it? Good show, man. Your support during the last contretemps was invaluable. And the information your network supplied helped us win the day that much sooner. Fair England owes a great debt to both you and Major Campe."

Cheers rang out as Wynn steered his friend's chair away from the steps to a side parlor, not the one being used as an infirmary, thank goodness, but where they could have a private reunion.

Bette woke up after one of Mrs. Reese's maids handed Wynn a vinaigrette to wave under her nose. She started wailing again—but did not unwind her arms from around Troy. She looked like she would never let go, in fact. The poor fellow might have survived the war only to be drowned by his old playmate's tears of joy.

"We thought you died four years ago," Wynn simply said as Troy patted Bette's back.

"I know, and I am sorry. The War Office thought it was better that way, that I could serve in a different capacity, incognito, especially since my parents had passed on and I had no one waiting for me."

"You have been a spy for four years, and no one knew it?"

"An intelligence gatherer," Troy corrected him. "And the old man was right. Your information helped swing the tide. But then I was injured last year." He gestured toward his legs. "I can get around on crutches, but not as easily."

"Then why the hell did you not come home?"

"No mobility to speak of, no career, no income, no property, for my brother got the manor. I had nothing to come home for."

"You had me, you great gaby!" Bette cried.

"And you have a modest fortune. The money you lent me, you know," Wynn said.

"That was no loan. You won it in a card game."

"We both knew you lost on purpose, so it was a loan. I vowed to repay it, with interest. I was lucky with the investments. Your half will keep the both of you in comfort 'til your dying day, which had better be at least fifty years from now, I swear."

"I'd heard you had the Midas touch. Do you truly mean to give me half? I merely gave you a paltry few hundred pounds."

"You gave me everything you had, man. I am only offering half. Contingent, of course, on your taking Bette off my hands. You do mean to marry the silly wench, don't you? As her, ah, temporary guardian, you might say, I feel I have to ask, you know."

The kiss his old friends shared was answer enough. Wynn left them alone and closed the door behind him.

He was poorer by half, but richer by twice in the things that mattered.

Chapter Twenty-three

Wynn was whistling as he walked down the hall. Not only did he have his friend home at last, to stay, but he finally had a credible witness to that duel. No one would doubt the word of Wellington's favorite when Troy vouched that Wynn had not fired early, that Lynbrook had walked off the field that fateful morning. As soon as Troy was settled, Wynn would have his man of business, his barrister, and the magistrate look into the matter. For now, Wynn was so happy, he actually felt like dancing!

On the way to the ballroom he was stopped by an aide to Wellington, who offered him a position with the War Office, without recompense, naturally. Now that he was merely wealthy instead of hideously rich, Wynn would have to think about accepting. From having nothing to do but count his money and watch it grow, he had a hundred ways to spend his time, all of them vastly interesting and important. He even had a friend with whom to share the decision. Troy and Bette would find a place in the country, no doubt, but he could go visit. They'd have children, and he would be a doting godfather.

Something was still missing from that rainbow-hued future he was painting, though. A whole corner, in fact, was blank, barren, empty. He already had a place in the country, dash it, and he'd be a good father, too. And a good husband. He walked with new purpose down the ballroom steps.

He did not get very far, for everyone, it seemed,
wanted to be his friend now. Wellington's commenda-
tion, and Bette wrapped in the major's arms, not
Wynn's, had sealed his acceptance. Even Marissa smiled
at him—and her face did not shatter from the effort.
Wynn cynically wondered if all these toadies would still
be as cordial if they knew he had promised away half
his fortune. He supposed his coffers were still full
enough for the mamas pushing their daughters at him,
and for the daughters pushing their chests out toward
him.

Was he supposed to pick a wife by the size of her
mammaries, like a milk cow? Her pedigree, like a horse?
Her dancing, like a trained bear?

He just could not do it, sift through their numbers and
pull out a jewel. For all Wynn knew about women, he'd
end up with fool's gold. Besides, the blondes were in-
sipid. The brunettes were boring. The raven-tressed chits
reminded him of witches.

He'd have a cigar instead.

Too many couples were strolling on the wide terrace,
likely looking for a dark corner where the chaperons
could not see them. Wynn stepped down onto a garden
path. That was more like it: a fine cigar, music in the
background, and no hopeful maidens in sight. Now he
could truly savor his night's successes. The failures, and
the females, would still be there tomorrow.

Then, out of the corner of his eye, he saw a glint of
gold disappearing down a different path. The trees were
strung with paper lanterns, but the gardens were still
dark. Perhaps he was wrong, just seeing a reflection from
the ballroom. No woman would be corkbrained enough
to go so far away from the crowds and the chaperons,
not unless she was trying to destroy her reputation.

Or trying out a gentleman's kisses.

Or meeting her lover.

It was none of his business; Lady Torrie had made

that very plain. If she had chosen to go husband-hunting in the dark, that was her father's concern, or her aunt's, not the suitor she had summarily rejected. No, he'd stay right here and smoke his cigar, which tasted like sawdust, and listen to the music, which must have stopped for the supper break. Besides, he told himself, there might be any number of women at the ball dressed in filmy gold fabric. The female might have been fat and forty, dressed as Galatea, trysting with a groom, for all he knew. He'd be a prime fool to follow them, a regular busybody and a marplot.

Whose feet were already headed down that path. Damn, but that woman could ruin a man's pleasure in life seven ways to Sunday.

Torrie's knight wanted to stroll the gardens, but she was not born yesterday. She was not going off alone with a strange gentleman, not even Sir Galahad. This gallant, on closer inspection, was far from the parfit gentil knight. In fact, his costume was so errant that it looked as if it had been collected from an old castle attic, in the dark. The visored helmet was meant to go with a full suit of armor, not a chain-mail tunic. The heavy wooden lance had been shortened until it could not have unseated a jouster unless he was on the same horse, yet still managed to trip Sir Jumble. The leather cross-gaiters looked more like horse harness, and the ornate, jewel-studded sword at his side was most likely made out of pasteboard. Other than asking her to walk with him, though, the knight had proved chivalrous enough, leaving her to her own thoughts while he worried at his heavy leather gloves.

Could she really be jealous of Lord Ingall's paramours? Torrie wondered. Was she merely trying to fool herself by declaring her moral disgust at his licentious behavior, when all she wished was to indulge in the same actions with him? The memory of his dark head so close to Lady Lynbrook's blond one, his eyes so concerned and attentive, was like a lance to her heart.

In fact, the knight's lance *was* pressed against her heart. "I do not find that amusing, sir," she said, meaning to walk past him back to the ballroom.

He poked at her again. "But you have pierced my defenses, fair goddess. I must have you."

"I am not on Mrs. Reese's menu, sirrah. You must be foxed."

"Nay, lady, I have never been more sober. I need you."

"Bosh." She pushed against the lance, batting it away, but the weight, and the knight's unwieldy gloves, caused it to drop. The heavy pole rolled off the terrace and down the steps into the gardens.

Torrie thought it a good thing that the silly visor muffled his words, for no *chevalier* used such language in front of a lady. Mrs. Reese's punch must have been more potent than she thought for this fellow to be so castaway this early in the evening. She started across the terrace.

"Wait, my lady, my goddess, please wait!"

She would not have, but his mitt was closed on one of her wings. She feared pulling the wing off, and half her gown with it, if she moved away.

"Please," he was saying, "won't you help me retrieve my weapon?"

"No, I am sorry, but my next partner will be waiting."

"It must be close by. Please."

"I cannot . . ."

"Oh, please. You see, I am ashamed to admit it, but I cannot bend over in this cursed costume. And these eye slits are hard to look out of."

"Then why do you not take the helmet off?"

"What, and ruin the unmasking after supper? Dear Mrs. Reese would never forgive me."

Dear Mrs. Reese would never forgive him for annoying one of her guests, but Torrie nodded. She could help fetch the knight his lance and be done with the ninny. So she went down the steps, the knight clattering behind her, and searched under the bushes for Sir Sot's stick.

"Here it is," she called, bending to retrieve the weapon. When she stood, however, the knight had his gloves off and his unsheathed sword pressing against her neck. The lance fell back to the ground with a thud.

The sword was steel.

She was alone with an attics-to-let knight in antique armor.

And her pistol was in her reticule, on the seat next to Aunt Ann.

Now who was the noddy?

Torrie opened her mouth to scream, but just then a cheer broke out in the ballroom. Most likely someone had made a betrothal announcement, or relayed glad tidings from the war. Perhaps the prince had arrived. All the other couples from the terrace were rushing for the doors, to go see. No one would hear her over the outburst.

"Just walk," the knight said, sounding completely sober.

The blood in her veins sounded louder, especially where the tip of the sword was pressed. She walked, away from the lights and the crowds, away from any hope of rescue. A few more steps and no one could hear her scream anyway, not over the ballroom noise. For the first time, Torrie was truly afraid. Not even that bobbing-block Boyce had threatened her with physical harm.

She could not just let him herd her along, like a pig to slaughter. The analogy made her shudder. She did not want to think about the villain's ultimate purpose in forcing her away from the party. Whatever it was, she was not going to like it. Therefore, she had to get away. Her mind was racing, even as she slowed her footsteps.

A weapon. She needed a weapon. But the lance was far behind, and Mrs. Reese's gardeners were much too efficient to leave dead branches around, or a shovel. She reached up to brush an errant curl from her cheek and caught a hairpin just as it was about to fall. Fine, now she had a means of defending herself—against an armored attacker with a sword! Torrie would have laughed, if she were not so near to tears.

Oh, where was her rescuer now? Please— No, she could not count on any kind of divine intervention again. This time she had to save herself. She collapsed, pretending to faint. The villain could not bend down. She could roll behind a lilac bush, then run like— but he skewered her gown to the grass with his sword.

"No more tricks, my lady. You are worth more to me alive than dead, but a few nicks and cuts won't make you less valuable. Now stand, slowly, and start walking again."

Well, at least she still had her hairpin, and now a handful of dirt in the other hand. If she could throw the dirt through those narrow eye holes, then she could pierce his bare hand with her hairpin. If he were injured, he'd drop the sword. If she picked up the weapon, she could . . .

Torrie doubted she'd be able to stab the man with his own blade, no matter how black his heart may be. Hitting him over the helmet would only give him a headache. So, she plotted, she would have to pick up the sword and run away with it, to keep it from him. Surely she could outrun a man weighted down with armor.

Thank goodness she did not have to rely on her chancy plan, for a tall, thin man was standing near an ornamental fountain. His mask identified him as another party-goer, for which Torrie thanked her lucky stars as she ran toward him.

"Help me!" she called out. "This dastard is threatening me at knifepoint! Thank heaven you are here."

The man reached out for her, and latched onto her arm. "Got her, gov. Just like we planned."

There were two of them? And Torrie had just begged

the second baseborn churl to save her? Life could not
be that unfair. And she could not be such an easy victim!
Well, this second slug-spit was not wearing any armor,
by Harry.

Just as he reached for a sack to put over her head,
Torrie tossed the dirt at his face. Then she stuck his
hand with her pin, as hard as she could. In her rage,
that was hard indeed. He howled and cursed, but let go
of her arm and the sack. Torrie grabbed the sack and
threw it at the knight's head, blinding him. He shouted
too, then raised the sword and swung it around in a wild
arc. Torrie ducked, but the flat side of the blade struck
his partner, who fell, lurching forward to crash into the
knight's knees. The dastard went down on top, sounding
like an avalanche of silver teapots.

Torrie ran.

Then she turned around and ran in the right direction,
back to the lights of the house.

Then she ran into a wall: the hard, well-muscled wall
of Wynn Ingram's chest. She was safe.

Chapter Twenty-four

"**W**hat, did your lover disappoint you?"

"My lover? You think that I . . . Oh, you oaf!" Torrie stepped back from Wynn's steadying arms and slapped him. "My lover, as you call him, abducted me at the point of his sword. He and his friend were going to stuff me in a sack!"

Before she could finish, Wynn's dagger was unsheathed and he was starting down the path. She called him back. "Don't bother. I heard them scrambling under the hedges at the rear of the garden as I ran. They must have had horses or a carriage waiting on the other side. They will be long gone by the time you get there."

"Hell and damnation. Are you all right?" Now that he was closer, he could see that her gown was stained and her hair was falling down her back and one wing was crumpled. He cursed again. Someone had dared to lay a hand on his goddess. Whoever he was, he was a dead man. "Did they hurt you?"

"No. Nothing to speak of anyway." Torrie knew she would have black-and-blue bruises by morning, but compared to what could have happened, she was fine. Or as fine as one could be, having been kidnapped, attacked, and then accused of meeting a lover.

"Was it Boyce?"

"I do not know. He was dressed as a knight in armor. It could have been, but I never thought Boyce meant to hurt me. The other man was too tall to be him."

"I'll find them. I swear it." Then he brushed the hair from her cheeks and cupped her face in his hands. "You are sure you are not injured?"

The tenderness evaporated her anger. All she had left was a trembling aftermath of emotions. She shook her head, no. "I was just so frightened, though."

He could feel her shaking, so enfolded her in his arms against his chest again. "Lud, I am a brute for thinking ill of you. And doubly so for letting my stupid suspicions keep me from going after you in time."

"But you were coming? That's why you were so far away from the house and the terrace?"

He pressed her closer even, so he could feel her heart beating beneath the thin fabric of her gown. "I was coming."

She sighed and stopped shivering, comforted as much by his words as by the warmth of his embrace.

When Wynn felt she had recovered somewhat, he asked her to tell him what had happened, if she felt up to it. Torrie nodded and told him about the clumsy knight and his lance, and how she could not cry out because of the noise inside.

"Wellington arrived," was all he said, thinking that she did not need to know about Troy and Bette at this moment.

"Mrs. Reese must have been in alt."

"She was. But go on. Where was the other man, and how did you manage to get free?"

She told him about the dirt and the hairpin and the sack, and he told her what a brave and brilliant woman she was.

The retelling, though, brought all the horror of the abduction back to her. Torrie could not help herself; she started weeping. "I was not brave at all," she said through her quivering lips, trying to hold back a sob. "I was terrified."

Wynn rubbed her back and let her cry, even though his opened shirt collar was no protection from the dampness. Hell, half the women in London seemed to cry on him. "That is even braver, sweetheart," he told her, "to act when fear makes you want to crawl into a little ball like a hedgehog, hoping that if no one sees you the terror will go away." He tried to straighten out the crumpled wing. "You did not give up, but you fought back despite the fear. You won, Torrie. You won."

She hiccuped and sniffled, and tried to smile at him. "I did, didn't I? I got away from two awful men with nothing but my wits to aid me."

"Two armed and dangerous men," he agreed. "Too bad you did not get to meet Wellington. He could have used you on his staff."

She gave a watery laugh. Wynn gave her his handkerchief so she could blow her nose and said, "But know this: if you had not escaped, if their strength was simply too great for even your ingenuity, I would have found you."

"You would?"

He nodded his head. "No matter where they took you or why. I did not save your life the first time to have some bounders steal you away."

"Oh, Wynn."

The sound of his name was both a sigh and an invitation. He took it. He took her lips and her doubts and her fears, and gave back strength and security and his own soul.

Torrie melted. There was no other word for how she felt. She softened and flowed and melded with Wynn, their lips, their breaths, their very beings. She forgot the horror, feeling only the magic of his kiss, the joy of their oneness.

But.

But they were not one, and she could not give herself to a man who was not her husband, and who also kissed any woman he could.

But they were at Mrs. Reese's costume party, not the Cyprians' Ball.

And he thought she took lovers.

So she slapped him again.

"Deuce take it, woman," he said as his head snapped back. "What was that for? You were kissing me, too, and enjoying it."

That was one of the reasons she'd ended the kiss: because she wanted it never to end, and she could not bear it if he were merely trifling with her affections. She could say none of that, though, not even to herself, so she said, "That was for not being there when I needed you." Then she saw the red mark she'd made on his face and started weeping again, ashamed and sorry and wanting to kiss the hurt away. "Oh, Wynn, I am so confused!"

Wynn rubbed his cheek. If Torrie thought *she* was confused . . .

Peculiarly enough, the footman asked Wynn if he was certain a surgeon was not required, after Wynn asked to have the Duchamp carriage brought 'round. The footman had not caught so much as a glimpse of Torrie, standing behind a column at the front of Mrs. Reese's house, and could know nothing of her *deshabille*. They had walked around the building through the side gardens, rather than face the ballroom and the pandemonium that would have ensued.

When Wynn sent another footman for Torrie's aunt and her cape, that servant looked him over carefully, as if for bruises, before setting off on his errands. London parties were obviously not the dull affairs they used to be.

As soon as Torrie was wrapped and bundled into the coach, her aunt at her side, Wynn went searching for her father.

Lord Duchamp was in the card room playing a desultory game of whist with three old friends who, like him, were only waiting for their womenfolk to decide they had had enough merriment. The earl looked up when

he saw the viscount, nodded at Wynn, then went back
to studying his cards.

One of the other gentlemen at the table said, "Remarkable evening, what, Wellington bringing your friend
back from the grave, eh?"

"Remarkable, indeed," Wynn agreed politely, then
addressed Lord Duchamp: "I need a word with you, sir,
concerning your daughter."

"My—" A grin broke over the earl's face. He took
Wynn's hand and began pumping it up and down. "I
was beginning to doubt she'd go through with it, what
with the evening growing so late. And you're the one
after all! I could not be happier, Ingall, let me assure
you. Why, I told the silly puss she would never find
one better!"

"My lord, I don't think you—"

"Of course, I cannot like this rumgumption of giving
away half your assets, lad, but we'll let the lawyers handle the details, eh? And it is not as if you could donate
the Ingall holdings to charity or sell off your estates to
repay a debt of honor, anyway. Entailed on your son, of
course." He beamed at the other cardplayers. "My
grandson."

The gentlemen at the table had been pretending not
to listen, but they were all smiling now, too. Before Lord
Elston could call for a toast, Wynn interrupted. "No, sir,
you mistake the matter. Lady Victoria is not feeling well
and wishes to go home."

Duchamp knocked his chair over in his haste. "Leave
a ball early? That is not like my girl. Why, I haven't had
any lobster patties yet. Waiting for the crowds to thin,
don't you know." He threw his cards on the table. "Gentlemen, forgive me. And forget anything I may have spoken out of turn."

Once they were away from the others, Lord Duchamp
said, "Now, tell me. You are looking like the devil himself. Is my girl all right?"

After hearing Wynn's account, Duchamp was all for calling out the Watch, the Runners, the army. Wellington was still at the ball, wasn't he?

"I think your daughter would prefer that no one knows about the altercation. If the gossips find out she left the ball with a gentleman, and returned with her hair down and her gown mussed, they will make much of it. I know what a bumble broth they can create out of air bubbles. This way no one has to know anything but that she went home ill, under her aunt's protection."

The earl huffed, and not just because of the pace Wynn was setting down Mrs. Reese's corridors. "I suppose you are right. Can't simply let the dastardly deed go unpunished, though. Then the scum will think they can steal young girls away at will. Do you think they were going to hold her for ransom?"

Wynn did not want to mention white slavers. "I have no way of knowing yet. I want to go look around the property, interview the stable hands and the grounds-keepers, to find out if they saw anyone acting strangely. Or stranger than masquerade guests usually behave. A knight in mismatched armor would have been distinctive enough that someone should be able to identify the bastard. Perhaps the butler recalls taking his invitation. I'll check."

"I'll help."

"I think you would be of more assistance to Lady Victoria at home, sir. She was badly frightened."

"Quite right. Deuce take it, I cannot think."

"Do not worry. I will make a thorough investigation. Just go home to your daughter. I'm afraid I sent her off in your coach, but I took the liberty of asking for the loan of one of Mrs. Reese's."

"What, did she charge you a new roof for some foundling home?"

Wynn smiled. "No, that goes on your bill."

Before stepping into the borrowed carriage, Duchamp

asked, "Do you think it was that chaw-bacon Boyce? I thought he wanted to marry the gal, not scare her half to death."

"Would you have given permission?"

"Not on your life."

"There is your answer. I will look into it."

Lord Duchamp took his hand. "According to Wellington, you are the right man for the job. But this time, lad, let the law handle the muckworm. Or me. We cannot afford to lose you for another six years."

Wynn made no promises.

Chapter Twenty-five

Wynn made no discoveries, either. The fallen lance told him nothing, nor the break in the hedges. No servants had seen anything out of the ordinary, except in the number of guests needing to be carried out of the ballroom. Mrs. Reese did not recall greeting such a knight's arrival, nor did Marissa, who as usual had made note of everyone at the ball, their pedigrees, predilections, and dance partners.

By mid-morning of the following day, though, Barrogi had the nickname of a petty criminal who fit Lady Torrie's description. "A tall broom of a *bandito*, they say, with straw-colored hair, who does not mind getting his hands dirty. Speaking of hands, *padrone*, someone said he was wearing a bandage on one of his mitts last night that was as big as a turnspit."

Wynn looked over at the dog sleeping by the fire. "As big as a turnip?"

"And he's been talking about the brass he'll be spending at Sukey Johnstone's bordello. Me, I think he has been cooking his chickens before they hatch."

"That's how you make eggs, dash it. What is his name?"

Barrogi shrugged. "They call him the Scarecrow, and no one could tell me, no matter how much of your money I spent on Blue ruin, *padrone*, where he slept. I know where he drinks, though." He finished cleaning his fingernails with his knife and slid it back up his sleeve. "This man, I think, has to disappear, no?"

"No. He has to be taken up so he can cry rope on the man who paid him. Lord Duchamp assures me the magistrate's office will cooperate fully, so I'll get them to round him up."

"And Signore Boyce?"

Wynn carefully placed his own sheathed knife in his boot. "Boyce has not been home in days. I checked. The duns are camped out there. It seems his valet left last week because he had not been paid for months."

"Aha! Do you want me to hire this unemployed valet for you?"

"Hell, no. He let Boyce prance around in puce stripes. Besides, I am managing."

With the aid of the laundress across town, the bootblack next door, and spotted kerchiefs, Wynn was getting by. He would not be going to any more balls, formal or fancy dress, not if he could avoid them. There was only one woman he wanted to dance with anyway. Right now he had to keep her safe, and nothing else mattered. "I'll tell the Runners to arrest this Scarecrow. He'll know where Boyce is, or where they were supposed to meet. Then we will be rid of the blackguard once and for all."

Barrogi shook his head. "You think your English courts will hang a titled *bastardo*? One of their own? Me, I think he goes free."

Wynn tucked his pistol in the back of his buckskins, beneath his coat. "Justice will be done."

Before he left to make sure all the safeguards he had ordered for Duchamp House were in place, Wynn tossed an extra coin to Barrogi. "Here, take Rosie for another ice, will you, so she does not get lonely. Tell her I have not forgotten her. In fact, Duchamp has this footman, Henry, who might suit her for a husband. I'll talk to him while I am there."

Barrogi stopped brushing his own coat to catch the

coin. "A lowly footman? For the *signora*? You don't drink champagne with boiled cabbage, do you?"

Wynn did not eat boiled cabbage. "Well, tell her I am thinking about a solution to her dilemma."

Barrogi smoothed the strands of hair across the front of his head and dabbed some of Wynn's cologne on his weathered cheeks. "You do that, *padrone*. You keep thinking."

When Wynn reached the front door of Duchamp House, after commending the cordon of wounded and retired veterans Major Campe had deployed there, he expected the hall to be dark and quiet. He expected Lady Torrie to be wan and shaken, perhaps resting from her ordeal. He expected a warm welcome. Hah.

The entry was in a swivet, servants darting hither and yon, and Lady Torrie was tying her bonnet strings, preparing to go out. Her color was bright, her hand was steady, and the glare she cast his way could have withered the wings off a stone gargoyle. "Come, Ruthie," she told her maid. "We must be on our way."

Wynn crossed his arms over his broad chest and stood with his back to the door. Most of the servants disappeared. "And where do you think you are going, my lady? Not even you could be so harebrained as to go traipsing off to the shops after nearly being abducted. Or is a new bonnet more important than your life?"

"Not even? Harebrained? How dare you!"

He raised his eyebrow. If the shoe fit . . . Besides, he'd dared worse—and been slapped for it. "I do not even see that footman, Henry, who was supposed to be with you at all times."

"What, when there is an army of ragged soldiers camped on my doorstep? The neighbors must think Papa is forming his own militia in preparation for Bonaparte's invasion or some such tomfoolery."

"The men are there for your safety, as you well know, to make certain no one enters the house or grounds."

"And are they also there to prevent me from leaving?"

"I believe I can handle that on my own." He leaned back against the wide oak door as if he were prepared to spend the day there.

"There are other exits, you know."

"Of course. And my men watching each of them."

He looked down, but it was not Homer who was growling. He smiled at the lady, who only stamped her foot.

"Who gave you the right to order my life, then? Tell me that."

Wynn's lips stayed quirked up in a half smile. "Fate, I suppose. That's what you said, anyway. You see, once a man saves a life, I have always been told, he is responsible for that person. As if he continues to hold the other's welfare in his hands."

"That is absurd." So was the blush Torrie could not conceal at the thought of being held in his hands. The infuriating man was looking as much like a rogue as he had when dressed as a pirate. And he was smiling like a mischievous boy. She crossed her own arms in front of her chest, to show that neither his charm nor his air of command held sway with her. "Furthermore, my errand is none of your business. It is not dangerous, not far afield, and not anything a man could understand."

Wynn did not budge. Torrie looked daggers at him. The butler discreetly disappeared. The maid whimpered. The dog wagged his tail.

Wynn shifted his gaze from the militant blue of Torrie's angry eyes to the maid's tear-reddened ones. She seemed just a bit older than her mistress, and a great deal less confident. His voice softened. "Miss Cobb, is it?"

The maid stared at her shoes. "Ruthie Cobb, my lord. Cobb will do."

"Well, Miss Ruthie Cobb, perhaps you would be kind

enough to reveal your destination, since your mistress seems too pigheaded to do so."

Torrie gasped, but before she could shush her abigail, Ruthie whispered, "Just across the square, to Lord Fraser's house."

Fraser was an old curmudgeon with an unsavory reputation. What the deuce could Torrie want with that dirty dish? "You don't think Fraser was the man who tried to steal you away, do you?"

Torrie was amazed that he'd think such a thing. "Fraser? What in heaven would he want with me? He will not have a woman in his house, and that is the problem. Now, please move so we can go about our business."

"Stand aside while you go calling on a loose fish you know will not receive you? When the visit would be highly improper if he did consent to an interview? Not on your life."

"You might as well tell him, ma'am," the maid conceded. "It's not as if everyone won't know soon enough anyways."

Torrie sighed. "Very well. Poor Cobb here, Ruthie, finds herself in an awkward situation." Instead of moving away from the door, the infuriating viscount simply raised that eyebrow and waited for her to continue. She sighed again. "Ruthie is breeding."

"Good grief, Fraser?" That was not what the *on dits* said about the old shabster.

"Of course not. One of his footmen, Cyrus."

"He promised to marry me, Cyrus did," the maid told Wynn. "Or I never would have . . . But now Lord Fraser won't give us permission."

"He won't let his servants wed," Torrie continued, "because, he says, he does not want any cuddling in the corners."

"We wouldn't!" Cobb swore.

Obviously they had.

"So what do you propose to do?" Wynn asked Torrie,

even as he stepped back and opened the door for the
two women to pass through.

Torrie did not bother commenting on the fact that
Lord Ingall seemed intent on accompanying them, and
his dog, too. Why complain about what one could not
alter? "Why, I propose to change Lord Fraser's mind,
of course. Barring that, I shall try to convince Cyrus to
hand in his notice. He should not be working for such
a dreadful man anyway."

Wynn gestured toward the soldiers in ragged uniforms
who were taking up positions to guard the little cavalcade. "Work is not easy to come by these days. Do you
intend to offer Cyrus a position in your household?"

Torrie had not gone that far. "I have not spoken to
Father about it yet. I know he will not permit Ruthie to
stay on as my maid, though. It will not look right, my
having an abigail who is having a child."

"I should say not, my lady!" Ruthie agreed.

"And Cyrus should have thought of that before he—"
Torrie did not complete the sentence, but she did complete her thought: "Men. Hmph."

"What about Miss Cobb? Did she have no say in the
matter? No thoughts about the future?"

"I suppose she ought to have," Torrie said, bringing
a scarlet blush to Ruthie's cheeks. "But now she is the
one carrying a babe and soon to be out of a position."

That was irrefutable. Homer lifted his leg on a bush,
seeming to speak for all of the silent party.

As they reached the other side of the park, about to
cross the street in front of Fraser House, Wynn said,
"You know, I have had great luck as a matchmaker
lately. I could give this mare's nest a go."

"You?" Torrie was incredulous.

"Yes, I have my sister-in-law's cousin well-nigh buck-
led, and I don't doubt Lady Lynbrook and my friend
Campe will be calling the banns soon."

Torrie had heard the talk. "You cannot take credit
there. They say the two were childhood sweethearts."

"Ah, but I paved the way," he said, thinking of the money.

Torrie was thinking of the duel. Heavens, what if Wynn offered a challenge to old Lord Fraser? "I do not think we will need your assistance."

They needed his shoulder to keep the door open when a grizzled old man with one clouded eye tried to shut it in their faces. "No women allowed. 'Specially ones what come without an invite."

Wynn could not help the superior smile he flashed Torrie's way as he told the old man, "We have not come to see Lord Fraser, but an employee of his named Cyrus."

"I be Cyrus," the servant replied. Torrie gasped and Wynn would have, but the man went on, scowling at Ruthie. "I suppose you want my son, Young Cyrus. Though what you want with the lad now, I don't know. Almost cost him his place already."

Young Cyrus was sent for, and the looks he and Ruthie shared could have melted even Lord Fraser's heart, if he had one. Before Torrie could open her mouth, Wynn asked the maid: "Do you love him, Miss Cobb?"

"With all my heart, milord."

"And you, Young Cyrus? Do you wish to marry Ruthie?"

"More'n life itself."

"Very well. Do you know how to perform the services of a valet?"

Young Cyrus looked at Wynn, at the loosely knotted kerchief, the scuffed boots, the dog hairs on his sleeve. "Better'n the man you've got now, I figure."

Torrie had to smile. In three seconds Wynn had changed a young man's life for the better. All Young Cyrus could have hoped for as a footman was to rise to take his father's place as butler, eventually. "But what about Ruthie?"

"She comes, too. If my sister-in-law ever relinquishes my town house, there will be a separate apartment for

Ruthie and the babe. In the meantime, I am in desperate need of a housekeeper in Kensington. It will be close quarters, but the pay is good. And a valet earns far more than a footman. Some seem to earn more than the king. What do you say?''

Young Cyrus said he would go upstairs and pack.

"Ruthie?"

"I hate to leave Lady Torrie, but I know I cannot stay. So thank you, my lord. I accept."

"Good. I'll see about a special license this afternoon." He smiled at the young woman. "We cannot have any illicit cuddling in my house, either, you know." Then he turned to Torrie. "What say you, my lady?"

"I say you are a very nice man, Lord Ingall, for a rake."

Chapter Twenty-six

"You wound me." Wynn put his hand over his heart in mock pain. But he really was hurt, that she could still think so poorly of him. Zeus, what would it take to make her trust him? Time, he supposed. Well, he had until Scarecrow and his employer were apprehended, for he did not intend to let Torrie out of his sight until he knew she was safe. He certainly could not trust *her* to keep out of trouble.

"No, I mean it," she was saying as they walked back across the park, a glowing Ruthie following but out of listening range. "Many rich men make donations to charity, but you truly care about helping people. I heard what you are doing for your friend, the major. I do not know another man who would have done the same."

"Troy would." Embarrassed, Wynn tried to make light of his actions. He wanted her to like him, by Jupiter, not think of him as a benevolent uncle. "Besides, I would never hear the end of it from Bette if she had to do without the latest gimcrackery."

"Do you mind?"

"About the money? Of course not. I have more than I can spend in nine lifetimes. And he deserves it, not just for the loan he made me, but for what he has given in the service to his country."

"No, I mean do you mind about Bette, Lady Lynbrook? About her marrying your friend?"

"Lud, no. As you said, they were childhood sweet-hearts. I was never . . . That is, we never . . . She never cared for anyone but Troy, and I never looked upon her as anything but a friend."

"Then why did you— No, it is none of my affair."

Wynn wanted to tell her to make it her affair. She looked so pretty in a pink gown he wanted to have an affair. Lud, it was all he could do not to kiss her again, right in the park in broad daylight. She would most likely skewer him on the tip of her parasol. It would almost be worth it. Instead he asked, "The infamous duel?"

Torrie nodded. If she could understand the past, per-haps she could understand the present, how a man could be a rotten acorn one minute and a strong, straight oak the next. Then she could make a guess about the future.

So he told her, how Lynbrook was a rotter who regu-larly beat his servants, his wife, his mistress. When in his cups, which was most days, he would strike out at anyone who crossed him, sometimes at anyone who merely crossed his path. Troy and Bette thought of run-ning away, but they did not have enough money to live on and nowhere to go. Lynbrook laughed at Troy and Wynn when they called him to account. They were mere boys, fresh out of university, with no power, no pressure to bring against him, no legal right to interfere. So they decided that Wynn would challenge him, since an illegal duel would destroy Troy's career.

Lynbrook did not accept the challenge, so Wynn made blatant overtures to the baron's wife, letting the gossips link their names. No self-respecting man could let such an insult go unpunished. Lynbrook could, he respected Wynn so little. It was not until Wynn stole Rosie away that he finally got Lynbrook's attention.

"We meant to teach him a lesson, not kill the dastard. At the least, we hoped to send him to his bed for a fortnight to recover from a minor wound, leaving Bette alone. I aimed for his shoulder. I hit his shoulder. Somehow he died."

"You don't know how?"

"Oh, he died from a gunshot wound to the heart, all right. The coroner said so. But my parents and brother shipped me out of England before I could find out who actually fired the shot. His valet swears he knew nothing about it, and Bette thought I had been trying to kill the makebate. Now that Troy is here to corroborate my story, the magistrate says he will send a Runner to interview the current Lord Lynbrook, the one who had the most to gain by the baron's demise. It had to be him or the surgeon, for once they were home, the household would have heard that second shot."

"Then you never fired early, or tried to kill him?" She answered herself: "Of course not."

Torrie's confidence in Wynn removed the earlier hurt. He took her hand and kissed the fingertips. She *did* like him. That was enough. For now.

Torrie's fingers tingled—right down to her toes. She wanted him to kiss her. That was never the problem. Every time she was near the man she could feel her body try to sway toward his. She wanted him, but she wanted him to be the right man, the one who would never betray her trust, who would never break her heart. She touched the jeweled key that lay there, over that fast-beating organ. She could love a rogue—she doubted her heart would listen to reason once it had chosen— but she could not marry one.

Torrie was desperately afraid it was Wynn or no one, but she needed time to tell. Therefore she made only token resistance when they reached her door and Wynn said, "I have to insist that you do not go out without proper safeguards."

She raised her eyebrow in imitation of his own expression of superior inquiry. " 'Insist'?"

Wynn smiled and brushed his fingers lightly over her

brow. "Request, then. I most humbly request that my lady not leave the house without adequate protection."

"And what do you consider adequate protection, my lord watchdog?" she asked smiling back.

"Why, me, of course. And Homer."

So in the following days, while the Runners searched for the Scarecrow, and Wynn and Barrogi searched for Boyce, the viscount, the earl's daughter, and Homer were seen everywhere together. Dressed in the first stare, finally, Wynn walked with Torrie in the park, attended the opera with her, and drove at her side out to Richmond for a picnic, well chaperoned by her maid and his new valet, who instantly disappeared into the maze there, leaving only the dog as dogsberry.

They viewed museum exhibits, Mrs. Reese's charity schools, and one of Wynn's ships, when it docked in the harbor. They went to a musicale at Lady Lynbrook's, and watched Major Campe turn Bette's pages, missing more than half the sheets as he watched her face instead of her fingers.

They even ate dinner at Wynn's sister-in-law's house. His house.

Wynn was relieved to see that Marissa had sense enough not to seat her gentleman's gentleman among the gentlefolk at her table. Marissa also had sense enough, once she noted how Wynn's glance kept lingering on Lady Torrie, and how Torrie could not restrain the soft smile when he was near, to start looking for a house of her own. Wynn would pay for it, of course.

Pages of wagers in White's betting book were conceded. The Keyes Diamond was as good as claimed. The new bets were on the dates of the nuptials and the birth of the first child. A few of the gamblers, watching how the couple kept brushing against each other, seemingly by accident, laid odds that the second event would not be the full nine months after the first.

The only question in everyone's mind was, What was taking them so long to send in the official notice?

Torrie's father was almost tearing his hair out, what he had left. He wanted to go home. He missed his wife. Letters from Yorkshire were not nearly good enough. Now that things were finally going so well with the youngsters, though, he did not want to precipitate another crisis by asking Wynn's intentions. Oh, the lad was honorable enough, Duchamp had no doubt, and brave enough to take on a strong-willed woman, but was Torrie convinced of his worth? He wrote another letter to his wife, begging her assistance.

Wynn was waiting for Torrie to ask him. After all, he'd asked her the last time and had been firmly rebuffed. Besides, he was waiting for a response from the magistrate's office, who was awaiting a report from the Runner who had gone to Lord Lynbrook's country residence. Wynn wanted his name exonerated once and for all before he offered it to Torrie again.

And there was still the problem of Rosie. Not only was that dilemma not going away, but it was growing larger daily. Any husband who could be purchased for her was wrong by definition, and a chancy fate to inflict on Rosie and her infant. But Wynn could not get engaged, hold a marriage ceremony, and go off on a bride trip, leaving poor Rosie to fend for herself.

Torrie was waiting to hear about Rosie, too. The child could not be his, she knew, since he had not been anywhere near England at the right time, but if Wynn intended to take up with the woman again, once she gave birth . . . Well, that did not bear thinking of, but Torrie could not help herself from doing just that.

Besides, they had both tacitly agreed to put off talk of the future until the kidnappers were found. What good was planning tomorrow while today was still so fraught with danger?

The Scarecrow was soon apprehended, but he would not reveal his employer's identity. He was going to be transported anyway, so why should he cooperate? Then his bandaged hand began to fester, so he traded Boyce's name for a surgeon's visit. He still kept mum about Boyce's new address, claiming he had no knowledge of it, or he would have gone there to collect his pay. Actually, the Scarecrow was hoping Boyce eventually got the witch who'd wielded the hairpin.

Barrogi was all for conducting an inquiry of his own, if they left him alone in a cell with the Scarecrow for a few minutes, but Wynn was not that desperate yet. The duns had moved into Boyce's old location, and the mawworm had not been seen since the night of the masquerade, but he had to appear somewhere.

Meantime, Wynn was enjoying himself. Not only was he getting to spend time with Torrie but his meals were hot, his bathwater was always ready, and he could see his reflection in his black boots. He never had to worry about being dressed right, and he never had to tie another blasted cravat. What a relief.

Torrie was not quite as content. Her father was looking harried, and her aunt was impatient to return to her own circles. She knew her name was being bandied about more than ever in the scandal sheets: the Dilatory Diamond, they were calling her, Miss Off-Keye. They all—the gossips, her family, and even the household staff—considered her overnice in her requirements. Former friends were giving her nasty looks, as if to say that if Torrie did not want the best thing to swim into their orbit, she should throw him back into the pool. Wynn did not seem to mind, but Torrie was growing uncomfortable. Besides, she needed a new maid.

The first one the agency sent, Fairfax, talked too much.

Constance Dawe could not sew a straight seam.

Miss Lightman— Oh, botheration. Torrie hired Tina, from Madame Michaela's.

The only other difficulty was the argument Torrie and Wynn had over where to hold the wedding breakfast. For Ruthie and Young Cyrus, of course. Torrie felt it should be at Duchamp House, at her father's expense. Wynn wanted to host it in Kensington, where the couple would be living. They settled on the Cricket Inn at the outskirts of town.

Wagons brought servants from Duchamp House and Fraser's place, and carriages brought the gentry: Torrie and her father, her aunt and Wynn. Fraser did not come, but Major Campe did, with Bette. Barrogi brought Rosie and Homer to give them both an outing, he said. Rosie and Bette wished each other well in passing. The menservants got up a game of cricket on the green, with Mallen and Old Cyrus arguing every call while the maids cheered them on. There was enough food and drink and private parlors and secluded walking paths to keep everyone in spirits for the joyful occasion.

When Lady Lynbrook and Major Campe, now on crutches, made their slow way down toward the duck pond, Lord Duchamp suggested that Wynn take Torrie down one of those tree-hung lanes, hoping that the newlyweds' happiness was catching. If he thought banging their heads together would knock some sense into them, he'd do that instead, by George. He'd be an old man, a bald, old man, before these two nodcocks came to an understanding.

Embarrassed at her father's obvious ploy, Torrie colored, but went off without the least hint of reluctance. If Papa knew that the bride was breeding, Torrie supposed, he'd be singing a different song, and keeping Torrie as far from Wynn, and temptation, as possible. Torrie had no intention of telling.

"Ruthie made a beautiful bride, don't you think?" she asked when they were away from the others. She could not help wondering what it would be like to carry a babe, Wynn's infant, inside her.

"They say all brides are beautiful on their wedding
day." Wynn could not help thinking how beautiful his
Torrie would be.

And her father could not help cursing when his daughter arrived back at the inn with no hair ribbon, no glove,
and no blasted engagement ring!

Chapter Twenty-seven

Lord Boyce was weighing his options. Even his scale was crooked.

He could not go home because the bailiffs were there. Everything of value had been sold off anyway.

He could not make another try for Lady Torrie because a small army surrounded her. She was too hard to handle anyway.

He could not be seen on the town because the Runners were there. Every heiress—lady or merchant's daughter—was out of his reach now anyway.

How the mighty were fallen! What he did have was a beard and soiled clothing, thanks to losing his valet, so he was not quite so recognizable in the shadows of the low taverns he was forced to frequent. He had the horse and wagon the Scarecrow had stolen, so he had a means of transportation, and he had a roof over his head. The roof leaked, and mice and spiders lived in it, but it had to be better than Newgate's. He also had enough blunt to see him to Scotland and his father's old abandoned hunting box, where no magistrate would think to look for him. The box was more a shack; he could barely understand the country lumpkins nearby; and he had no monies to live on once he got there.

So it was starve in Scotland or languish in a London jail. Or make one last attempt at kidnapping.

The whole disaster was Lady Torrie's fault. If she were not so beautiful, so rich, and so well-connected, he would never have settled on her in the first place. Why, he could have fallen in love with any other chit's face and fortune if the Keyes woman had not smiled at him now and again. Dammit, if she had married him like a sensible female, he never would have considered a life of crime. He'd be dressed in elegance and seated in the lap of luxury, instead of sitting on the floor of an abandoned cottage in rags, trying to start a fire in the smoking hearth. Lady Victoria Keyes had caused the mess, so she should pay. That made perfect sense to Lord Boyce. Unfortunately, he could not think of a way to make the wench supply him with enough funds to establish a new life in the lavish style to which he deserved to be accustomed.

Then he heard about her and that encroaching Ingall. Even in the dives they were talking about the Diamond's hero, and the Nabob's Jewel. Hell, the man was barely a gentleman, he dressed like a barbarian, and he did not even need the Duchamp blunt! Life was so unfair Boyce almost cried, except that would dampen his tinder. But now he thought of a way to get his money and his revenge both.

The viscount had to be worth something to the Keyes woman. He had to be worth a lot more to that lucky soldier friend of his they were talking about, especially if all the papers were not signed yet handing over half the fool's fortune. Then there was that starchy sister-in-law. She'd pay just to keep an abduction quiet. Hell, Boyce figured, he would not even have to send out ransom notes. Ingall could simply write a note to his own man of business to have the blunt delivered. Any fool who was dicked in the nob enough to give away half his brass deserved to be relieved of the rest, for his own protection. Yes. Boyce could capture Lady Torrie's blasted champion.

There were three things wrong with Boyce's plan: Ingall was bigger than he was, stronger than he was, and, Boyce feared, smarter than he was. Of all Boyce's

choices, suicide was his least favorite. He may have
made a few minor miscalculations in the past, Boyce
told himself, but he was neither stupid enough nor crazy
enough to take on a real-life hero.

So he'd kidnap Ingall's dog.

The viscount had to be the softest touch in all of London, Boyce decided, giving his blunt to charity, hiring
all those filthy soldiers, taking in every stray off the
streets, to say nothing of running into burning buildings
to rescue perfect strangers. Surely he'd pay a king's ransom for the return of his mongrel, for the flat was sel-
dom seen without the fleabag. Boyce would not have
spent a groat to ransom his own mother, but each to his
own, and Ingall's own into Boyce's pockets.

Now, stealing a dog, especially a small dog, ought to
have been a snap for an astute fellow like Boyce, Boyce
thought. Why, it might not even be a crime. He could
say the mongrel followed him home. A sausage, a sack,
and a string—that was all he'd need, and he already had
the sack and the rope they were going to use to tie up
the heiress. The only thing missing was the damn dog.
Ingall never let the cursed canine out alone. You'd think
it was a blasted baby instead of a mere dog, the way
Ingall toted the thing around with him. When the viscount did leave his lodgings without the creature, someone else was always in the place, a maid or the valet or
that foreign fellow who picked his teeth with a stiletto.
Boyce was not in a hurry to take up housebreaking,
not there.

He added a golden boy to the ransom he was going
to ask, for having to part with another precious coin just
to find the address. What kind of Croesus lived in such
an unfashionable part of town anyway? Boyce was more
than convinced the viscount was attics to let when he
saw the shabby residence.

He saw Ingall walk the dog early in the morning, and
he saw him walk it late at night. Great gods, did the
man not understand that was what servants were for?

Boyce could not wait any longer. His money was dwindling, along with his patience. Besides, since his pockets stank of sausage, strange dogs had taken to following him around. He revised his plan.

First he grabbed one of the street dogs. After he bandaged his hand, he was more selective, coaxing the second stray with a bit of sausage. It ran off before he could get the rope around its neck. The third mongrel was too old to run and too tired to care. It was missing an ear, half its tail, and some of its teeth. For a bite of the sausage, it would have followed Boyce to hell and back.

So Boyce slipped a noose around its neck and pulled his slouch hat down low on his forehead. He pretended to be out for a stroll, pretending the club in his hand was a walking stick, and the ugliest creature in the world was his faithful companion. When he saw his quarry walking toward him, he touched the brim of his hat.

"Mornin'. Nice dog, that."

Wynn nodded politely and paused while the two dogs investigated each other. "A, uh, handsome chap you have there, too." He moved on, whistling for Homer to come along.

Boyce waited, then followed. When Ingall reached the end of the block, headed toward the gardens, Boyce pulled the old dog faster. No one was in sight, no one would hear any outcries. He wasn't sure what he was going to do, but it was now or never.

It was never for the old dog. The sausage was gone, and he had no hurry left in him. He lay down. Boyce pulled, the dog snarled. Boyce pretended he had more sausage in his hand. The dog bit him. Boyce raised his club. "Why, you miserable, worthless—"

"I say, is there a problem? Your dog appears to be sick." Wynn bent down to examine the ancient mutt.

And Boyce brought the club down on his head.

He had done it! He had actually succeeded in separating Ingall from his pet. Things were finally going his

way. Boyce almost danced with joy, except he still had
to catch the little ratter.

There was the dog, jumping around out of arms'
reach, snarling and showing its teeth . . . and there was
Ingall, stretched out cold on the ground. Boyce's wagon
was close by. The dog . . . or Lady Torrie's lover? It
was a hard choice, all right.

Wynn awoke with Satan playing cymbals in his skull.
He tried to rub his aching head, but discovered that his
hands were tied behind him. His feet were tied to the
legs of the battered chair he sat on.

He grimaced against the pain and made his eyes look
around. He was in a hovel of some kind, cold, dark, and
dirty, with little furniture beyond his chair and a littered
table. Someone had obviously been here recently, for
the grease stains were fresh and the wine in one of the
chipped glasses had not yet dried. The ashes in the fireplace still smelled of smoke, although no new fire had
been laid. He twisted around and spotted another room,
but could not see past the doorway.

"Hey," he called out. "Who is there?"

No one answered. The front door was shut tightly, but
the windows were not covered, so his assailant must not
be worried about neighbors peering in. It was still daylight, but gray and overcast, so Wynn could not tell the
time by the sun's position. He could hear no peddlers'
calls or carriage wheels, so guessed he had been taken
somewhere on the outskirts of London, deuce take it.

Cudgeling his brain, he recalled a cudgel, in the hands
of a shabby old man with a broken-down dog. Why the
devil the man would attack Wynn, he had no idea. All
he knew was that he was going to kill the bastard who
did this.

First, of course, he had to get loose. He could bounce
along in the chair until he reached the table, he supposed, then break one of the bottles somehow, and saw

at his bonds—and his wrists—with a shard of glass. His
head pounded at the thought. Besides, Wynn might not
be able to tie a neckcloth worth a tinker's damn, but a
rope, a cord, a length of hemp? Given enough time,
there was not a knot he could not untie, be it on a ship,
in a warehouse, at a wilderness trading post. The fact
that the knots were behind his back added a mere minute or so to his efforts. He appreciated the challenge,
for it took his mind off the pain in his brainbox.

Wynn's captor, it seemed, was as bad at tying knots
as he was at housekeeping. The ropes at the viscount's
hands fell away in two shakes of a dog's tail—if the
knave who struck Wynn hurt Homer, he would die
twice—and the ones at his feet instantly followed.

He stood gingerly, then waited for the room to stop
spinning. He appeared to be in one piece, except for the
gash on the back of his head. The blood was already
dry, so he must have been here for some time. His gun
was missing from his waistband, and his purse was gone
from his inner pocket, but Wynn's knife was still in his
boot, another mark of the assailant's ineptitude.

The other room held one cot with two ragged blankets
and a chair with clothes draped over the back. On the
seat rested a visored helmet. Inside the knight's head-
piece Wynn found a tin of tooth powder, a comb, and a
dented silver button—with a B engraved on it.

Very well. Boyce. Wynn had not thought the fop had
the brass to attack someone who could fight back. Of
course, he'd taken Wynn by surprise, from behind, with
a bat, but Wynn was still impressed. He'd still kill the
bastard, but with a modicum more respect.

When? That was the question. He could leave now,
hail the first passing cart to take him home, round up
his band of armed men to come surround the place, and
notify the magistrate while he was at it. Everything
would be legal, by the book. They could arrest Boyce,
charge him with any number of crimes—and then let him
go. He was a lord, and the nobs did not hang their own.

Besides, Wynn did not know where he was nor how far from help. By the time he reached home, Boyce could have returned, seen his captive gone missing, and fled. To try another day, perhaps going after Torrie again. The idea of Boyce on the loose, and Torrie with nothing but a silly straw bonnet between her and his club, made Wynn's blood run cold. One drop of her blood and— How many times could one snake die?

Wynn wanted this ended now. Here. He wanted to get on with his life, with Lady Torrie Keyes in his life. So he did what he'd had to learn that first winter in the Canadian wilderness to keep from starving, when it was either hunt or be hunted. He used the rope and the table and the door and the fireplace poker to build himself a rabbit snare. Only a whole lot bigger.

Then he sat back in the chair, his hands loosely behind him holding the knife, and he waited. He had learned that, too.

Chapter Twenty-eight

Wynn was expected at his solicitor's office at nine of the clock to sign papers with Troy and Bette.

He was expected at Bow Street at ten, to hear the report from the Runner who had spoken with the current Lord Lynbrook.

He was expected at Duchamp House at eleven, to accompany Torrie and her father to look at two mares in foal he was considering purchasing.

When the usually prompt viscount did not arrive at any of his destinations, everyone began to worry. By twelve, they had all converged at the Kensington house, where Young Cyrus was equally as concerned. His lordship had never returned from his early morning dog walk, to don apparel suitable for paying important calls. His first weeks on the job, Young Cyrus fretted, and his employer would look like a ragpicker out in public. How was he to get respect at Shay's Tavern if his gentleman did not befit the title? Ruthie was upset that the viscount's breakfast had gone untouched. So had Homer's.

And Barrogi was missing, too.

"If they are together there is no need to worry," Troy said. He patted Bette's hand in reassurance.

But Young Cyrus reported that the Italian had been out most of the night, was asleep when the viscount left, and then departed, leaving a folded note behind.

"What did it say?" Bette asked, but Young Cyrus was

affronted that they might think he would read his employer's personal mail.

"Give it here." Lord Duchamp had no such qualms, and the Runner, worrying that some foul deed was afoot, thought he should read the note. Torrie was ready to grab the letter, if it would lead them to Wynn, but the solicitor, Castin, held out his hand. "As his lordship's man of business, I believe I should be the one."

He put on his spectacles, then held the letter closer, trying to decipher Barrogi's handwriting. "Oh, dear," he said, while everyone held their breaths. Castin looked to the Runner when Barrogi admitted taking money and a diamond stickpin from his lordship's dresser. Barrogi wrote that he intended to pay the viscount back when he opened his gambling parlor, the Four Aces, or the Winning Hand, in honor of his former employer, but Castin did not think that would hold weight with the representative of the law.

"Oh, heavens," Castin said, glancing at Lady Lynbrook when he read how Barrogi had run off to Gretna Green with Rosie Peters, his lordship's other former mistress, because Rosie deserved some romance in her life. He could not mention such a female in front of either of the ladies, much less read aloud how Barrogi would happily raise the woman's *bambino* as his own.

"Oh, my stars," Castin said, looking at Lady Victoria this time, when Barrogi wrote about leaving the viscount a wedding present. No betrothal notice had been sent to him to post.

"Oh, hell, hand over the demmed letter." Lord Duchamp was not one to stand on ceremony. He read it out loud from start to finish, which, happily, finished with the address of the Scarecrow's erstwhile partner in crime, Lord Boyce. Barrogi, it appeared, had paid the felon a visit in prison as a parting gift for the viscount. He was sorry he could get no more details other than an abandoned cottage toward Islington, for the prisoner's jaw had somehow become broken.

Everyone rushed for the door and their horses and carriages and curricles, except for the weeping Lady Lynbrook, whom Major Campe refused to take along. Torrie did not wait for her father's groom to hand her up into the sporting vehicle. She almost did not wait for her father, either, snatching up the reins before he was seated. She whipped up the horses and wheeled the carriage while he held onto his hat.

"Here, now, puss," the earl shouted. "These are my prime cattle, by Jupiter." And well behaved enough that he trusted his well-trained daughter at the ribbons, to a point.

"But Wynn is in trouble, Papa. I know it."

The earl was worried, too. Ingall had not known that dastard Boyce's direction when he set out to walk the dog. Nor had he notified the Runners, or the soldiers who surrounded Duchamp House. Ingall's friend Major Campe could not have ridden *ventre à terre* to his aid, but Barrogi would have. The viscount had not known that his man had eloped, but he had not sent for him, nor sent excuses for missing his appointments.

Duchamp patted his daughter's shoulder anyway. "He'll be fine, poppet. Why, your lad has brought down bears and tigers, bandits and pirates. Do you think a counter coxcomb like Boyce could stop him?"

"If Boyce had a gun, he could." She called to the horses to pick up their pace. She could feel the danger, feel the threat, almost like a badly sewn seam on a gown or a toothache. Only now she had nowhere to rub to make the hurt go away. If something happened to Wynn, the pain would never leave her.

"I mean to marry him, Papa."

"I should hope so, after the way you two have been disappearing into dark corners at every chance. I don't know what your mother would say about such fast behavior." Well, Maggie would likely say they should leave the young people alone and go find their own private place. The earl hoped so, anyway, because he had been

leaving the youngsters unchaperoned, despite his sister
Ann's affronted complaints.

"But I will not be marrying him because of that silly
vow, you know. I meant it at the time, of course, that I
would wed the man who saved me, but what if he had
been the crossing sweep or a shoeless beggar?"

"I would have given him a reward and sent him on
his way."

"Exactly. And I will not wed Lord Ingall for a silly
whim, either, or just because you want me married so
you and Mama can be reconciled."

That seemed a deuced fine reason to Lord Duchamp,
but he held his peace, the same as he held his impatience
to take the reins back. "So why are you going to marry
the chap, then, my girl? Not for his looks, for I don't
relish my grandchildren having that hawk's beak for a
nose."

"Wynn has a beautiful nose," Torrie protested. "It is
very distinguished."

Lord Duchamp snorted, which caused the horses to
break stride, but Torrie had them back to speed in seconds. The earl said, "And you'll not wed for his money,
either, I'd wager, since you've fortune enough of your
own. Besides, the nodcock is liable to give more of his
away before you get him to the altar."

"I do not care, Papa. I would marry him if he gave
every shilling away. I love him, you see."

"Of course you do, puss."

"And I will forever."

Lord Duchamp nodded. "Just like your mother and I.
That's what we always wanted for you, my dear. That
same kind of lasting love."

"But he does not know."

"He knows. If I am certain of anything, it is that he
shares your regard."

"I never told him."

"You had your reasons, I suppose."

"The time was never right. But, Papa, what if Boyce

has hired other ruffians? You know Wynn will fight back. What if they kill him? What if I never get to tell him? Oh, Papa, I would die, too, I think."

Lord Duchamp took the whip out of his daughter's hand and cracked it over the horses' ears.

They were far ahead of the others when they reached the outskirts of Islington. Torrie slowed the horses and looked around helplessly. The area seemed deserted, the road forked up ahead, and the afternoon light was waning.

"Don't worry, puss. Campe will get here with his former soldiers, and they'll cover every inch of the place. The Runner fellow can demand information, and Castin will pay any ransom demanded. We'll have your lad back before the cat can lick her ear."

But it was a dog licking his sore foot near the right fork that caught Torrie's attention. She pulled the horses to a sudden stop, to her father's complaints about their tender mouths, handed him the reins, and jumped down. "Homer! It is you!"

The little dog wagged his tail. He'd gone as far as he could, then waited by the side of the road, confident that his master would return for him. Torrie picked him up and brought him to her father's curricle, placing the filthy dog on the seat, despite her father's frowns.

By now the Lynbrook carriage and the solicitor's gig, the mounted soldiers and the hackney with Young Cyrus and the Runner, had all caught up to them.

"Give the dog a drink," Major Campe called out from his coach, "and then put him down. We'll see where he goes."

One of the soldiers hurried over with a flask, and Lord Duchamp begrudgingly sacrificed his beaver hat for a bowl. Young Cyrus brought over some of the sliced ham Ruthie had pressed on him in case the master was hungry, having missed his morning meal and now his nuncheon. The Bow Street officer left his hired carriage and held out a bit of cheese left over from his own meal.

So many people had not watched an animal eat since

feeding time for the lions at the Royal Menagerie. Homer paid them no mind. He wolfed down the meat, swallowed the cheese without chewing, and gulped down the water. Then he belched indelicately. Young Cyrus handed him down from the curricle seat to Torrie, who patted Homer's head before setting him on the ground.

The soldiers dismounted; the earl held his restive pair in check; Torrie gathered her skirts, ready to follow the ragged terrier. Everyone held their breaths.

Homer raised his head and sniffed. He lowered his nose to the ground and sniffed again. Then he headed farther along the right fork in the road. .

"By George, the little fellow's got it!" Lord Duchamp said to no one in particular. "He could give my hounds a run for their money, I'd wager."

But Homer merely lifted his leg against a fence post, then sat down to lick his foot again.

"Damn," the earl declared, seconded by more than one of the watchers.

"No, I think he means us to follow," Torrie said, hurrying to pat the dog on his head again in encouragement. "Or to follow this line of fence, anyway."

"There is a house up ahead," Mr. Castin called from the seat of his gig. "I can just make out the chimney over those trees."

The former soldiers remounted and took their weapons out of their saddlebags. The Runner removed his pistol from his pocket. Young Cyrus went back to the hackney to fetch the meat cleaver he'd taken from the Kensington house kitchen. Major Campe had a rifle resting out the open window of the Lynbrook coach. And Torrie started walking, the dog at her side.

"My lady, Ruthie'll have my hide, iffen anything happens to you, an' the master will, too," poor Young Cyrus said, trying to get in front of her with his meat cleaver. She glared him back beside her.

"You get back in this curricle, girl," her father ordered. She did not hear him.

"Ma'am, you had ought not be here at all," the Runner said. "You are interfering with the law, so stand back." She did not heed him.

None could stride ahead, or drive on, or ride in front, because the dog was limping along at his own speed, sniffing as he went. No one dared to chance destroying the scent Homer was following, for there were narrow cart tracks leading in other directions, another group of chimneys now visible. Investigating each of those paths could take hours, and Lord Ingall had already been missing for far too many.

So they marched at a small, weary dog's pace, this most peculiar cavalcade.

What if the dog was following the scent of a rabbit? Torrie worried. Homer was no hunter. He was not much of a dog, but Wynn loved him, so she did. "Find him, my friend. Find your master. Find Wynn."

In another few yards Homer raised his head, perked his ears, and started trotting. When the path curved, he darted under a bush, and Torrie cursed, but he reappeared up ahead. The Lynbrook carriage was having difficulty as the roadway narrowed, but she could hear Major Campe urge his driver onward. And then she saw the old rickety house—and Wynn, seated outside in an old, rickety chair. The dog raced forward.

Wynn put his pistol back in his waistband when he recognized the rescuers. He stood and said, "I knew you would come."

He said it to the dog.

Chapter Twenty-nine

Wynn nodded toward Major Campe in the carriage and the mounted soldiers, in unspoken thanks for their intended assistance. He nodded toward Lord Duchamp in the curricle, the solicitor in the gig, and his own valet, one eyebrow raised as if to ask how much help they all thought he needed. Then he nodded toward the Bow Street Runner. "And I was hoping you would come."

He had acknowledged everyone but Torrie, who was covertly scrutinizing him for damage. "What about me?" she asked.

He put down the dog. "You? I prayed my wife-to-be would have enough sense for once to stay where she belonged." But his smile belied the words, and his open arms were an invitation Torrie had no intention of resisting. She ran into his embrace, saying, "Your wife? Oh, Wynn, I love you, too."

"Whew," her father said, mopping at his brow. "At least that's taken care of."

What remained was to take care of Boyce.

Wynn had not been able to kill the blighter.

Boyce had been crying, for one. It was hard to dispatch a man who was as sodden as a six-year-old.

He'd been unarmed for another. Well, he did have weapons before he dropped them, but Boyce could not reach them, caught in Wynn's trap and hanging upside down by his ankles as he was, like a haunch of venison strung up to age. Wynn found he could not kill a man who was threatening him with a whine instead of a knife or a loaded pistol or a club.

Boyce was not worth chancing another exile for, either. Boyce was still a titled lord, and the government was still run by titled gentlemen. They did not take kindly to having their ranks thinned by assassins, no matter how justified, for it reminded them too forcibly of their unfortunate counterparts in France. Wynn had too much of a future in England now to repeat his past mistakes. A few weeks ago he could have taken the first ship to anywhere. No more.

So he had not been able to butcher the blackguard. He had not been able to sit inside and listen to a grown man weeping, either, or suffer the stench of sausage that enveloped Boyce like a dirty shirt, an odor the rum touch also exuded. So Wynn had taken his chair outside, along with his pistol recovered from the caitiff's sack, and the meal Boyce had bought with Wynn's purse. If no one came soon, Wynn had decided, he'd have to load the stinking, sniveling scum in the old wagon and head back toward town. Now Boyce was the Runner's problem, as a representative of the Crown.

The soldiers were cutting the blubbering Boyce down from the rafters.

"It is better this way, my lord," the solicitor was saying, "letting the law handle such distasteful matters. They might not hang him, but I doubt one such as he will survive prison."

Lord Duchamp had other ideas, and his whip in his other hand. "He threatened my family."

Boyce started wailing. He tried to catch Lady Torrie's eyes, to plead to the only woman present. "But I love you! I did it all for you, because I could not bear to be apart from my beloved."

Wynn grabbed him by the throat and lifted him off the ground while the Runner pretended to catalog the armor helmet as evidence. "Beloved?" Wynn asked, shaking Boyce like a mud-encrusted rug. "You do not know the meaning of the word. What kind of love is it that could harm a hair of their beloved's head, or could make her suffer for an instant? Love is supposed to be selfless, you ass, and I doubt you've had a selfless thought in your entire sorry life." He threw the smaller man away from him, into the arms of two of the soldiers.

Boyce was not finished yet. He appealed to Major Campe, who had made his slow way to the door. "But . . . but I am a gentleman. I demand satisfaction of Ingall." Who knew what he could do with a pistol in his hand?

The major spun on his crutches in disgust, giving Boyce his back. "You have proved you are no gentleman."

But Torrie stepped away from Wynn's side, closer to Boyce, and said, "How dare you even think to challenge Lord Ingall, the man whose skull you almost crushed?"

Wynn tried to pull her back. "Hush, sweetings. My head is harder than that, I promise you."

Torrie was too enraged to listen to him. She shook her fist in Boyce's face and said, "You want satisfaction, you son of Satan? Well, so do I. You plotted to steal me away from my family, marry me against my will, and hold me for ransom. You almost made me Wynn's widow before I am his bride, to say nothing of almost killing both of us in that fire. Satisfaction? Sending you to prison does not half satisfy me, you disgusting, driveling little man." She hauled back her fist the way her father had taught her and clobbered Lord Boyce on the nose. The soldiers let him slide to the ground as Torrie rubbed her knuckles on her skirts. "Now I am satisfied."

Wynn pulled her outside, but not before telling the half-conscious Boyce that he was a lucky man. The lady could have basted his ballocks, too.

Lord Duchamp looked proud, but the major told his friend to tread carefully. "I would hate to see you in that woman's black books."

Wynn leaned over to whisper in his friend's ear as he passed: "I'll be safe. She loves me, you know. And she wants children. My children."

Lord Duchamp let Wynn and Torrie drive the curricle home while he rode with the solicitor. It was never too soon to start negotiating the marriage settlements, he felt. Besides, how much trouble could the pair get into, in an open vehicle, with a dog sitting between them?

He had not counted on them stopping along the way. Every half mile. Every ten minutes. Every time they needed to reassure each other of their love, their safety, how soon they could be wed, and who was the better driver. Besides, the dog needed to get down after all that food.

At one such stop, after Torrie had checked Wynn's skull for the third time, to make sure he was not bleeding again, and he had kissed her knuckles again, to ease the soreness from striking Boyce's nose, she explained about Barrogi's letter. Then she asked, "Do you mind?"

"What, that you opened my private mail? I hope you do not intend to make a practice of it, woman. No man wants a prying wife."

Which meant another stop, another kiss, another burst of joy that Wynn wanted a wife at all, and he'd found the perfect one.

"I suppose I can forgive you this time, for the letter did tell you where to look for me."

"No, do you mind about Barrogi?" Torrie asked, retying her bonnet strings.

"What, that the old rapscallion is gone? Zounds, no. He was of no use to me, and his talents were wasted as my assistant."

"No, silly. I mean do you mind that he eloped with Miss Peters?"

"Lud, I should say not. I did everything but buy them the ring and a license. I threw them together every chance I could."

Torrie was confused. "I thought you were looking for another husband for her."

Wynn laughed. "If I had mentioned marriage to Barrogi, he would have scampered off as fast as his legs and my money could carry him. But as long as it was his idea . . ."

"Hmm. Rosie Barrogi. It has a kind of ring to it."

"As long as she has a ring on her finger, I do not care. Speaking of which, do you prefer the family emerald engagement ring, if I can pry it away from Marissa, or a ring of your own, a diamond for my Diamond?" He smiled and pulled her into his arms for a long kiss.

Torrie gave up and tossed her bonnet to the floorboards, where the dog curled up on it to go to sleep. "Whatever you decide," she said, sliding closer to him on the seat, content at the very idea of his ring on her finger. "Do you think they will be happy?"

"Plucking pigeons at their gambling club? Delirious. But not as happy as we will be, my love."

Which necessitated another stop, another kiss. When they got underway again, Wynn's kerchief had joined Torrie's bonnet on the floor.

"I forgot to ask," Torrie said, and no wonder, with the wonder of Wynn's love, "what was the message from the Runner? Had he spoken to Lord Lynbrook? The current one, of course, Francis."

Wynn nodded and brought his attention back to the horses. "Yes, he saw the man, and finally got him to tell a new version of the story. What else could Francis do with Major Campe's sworn affidavit staring at him? What he says now is that when they got Frederick into the coach, he insisted Francis go back for his Manton, which he must have dropped during the duel when he was shot. The pistol was still primed—I know he never fired, so it must have been—so Francis tried to unload it. In the moving carriage. The damned thing had a hair trigger, of course."

"But why did he never say so?"

Wynn shrugged. "Because he was too much the coward to admit that he'd killed his own brother, even if by accident. It was easier to pay the surgeon to emigrate and blame me. He convinced the authorities to press charges, and I was gone, with no one the wiser."

The word Torrie used was one her mother had never taught her. "So what will happen to him now?"

"What can happen? He cannot give me back the lost years or my family's regard."

"That's it? Francis will simply get away with blackening your name?" Torrie was furious.

"What would you have me do, my love, challenge another Lord Lynbrook? Besides, he has three children."

"I thought the current Lady Lynbrook had two sons."

"Ah, but his mistress has a daughter. But do not fear, my bloodthirsty little bride, justice will be done. Lynbrook's confession will be made public. He will never show his face in London again, never cross my path. And that Lynbrook estate where we all met, near Bette's family property and Troy's father's manor, is not entailed. My man checked. I think that would make a fine wedding gift for Major and Mrs. Campe, do not you?"

"I think you are the finest, most generous man I have ever known."

"Don't forget the luckiest, my dear."

"Then you do believe in luck? I know you said it was foolish of me to believe in Fate, but could it not be possible that we truly were meant for each other, that some grand plan had decided we would suit?"

"How can we know, love? But just to make sure, I will make a contribution to the church, and lay flowers at the feet of the Cupid fountain you have in your garden. I will burn incense and sacrifice a hen at a standing stone. I'll do whatever it takes to give thanks, for giving you to me. And to you, for letting me love you."

It was a good thing the horses were beginning to recognize the way home and wanted their feed, for no one's hands or minds were much on the ribbons.

After an interval that would have sent the lady's father into apoplexy, Torrie withdrew the gold and diamond key from the chain at her neck. "Here," she said, tucking the charm into Wynn's pocket. "I will not need this anymore. You unlocked my heart, forever."

"And you are the key to mine, my love."

Somehow, and just before Lord Duchamp sent the soldiers out again to look for his cattle—and his daughter—they reached Duchamp House.

"Home," Torrie said with regret.

The Grosvenor Square mansion was not Wynn's home. Neither was the Kensington place, nor yet Ingram House or his country seat. But for the first time since he could remember, in Torrie's arms, Wynn was home at last.

Chapter Thirty

The wedding was perfect, all blooms and birdsong and tears of happiness in the Keyes family chapel in Dubron, Yorkshire. A little dog with a bow around his neck waited by the door. The groomsman leaned on his crutches by the altar, smiling at his friend's nervousness. Troy had been through the same thing not so long ago. "She'll come, Wynn. Stop worrying."

Then there she was, his bride, his love. Wynn did not wait for Lord Duchamp to reach the alter. He met them halfway down the flower-strewn aisle, and took Torrie's hand in his, so Cousin Deanna's husband could perform the short ceremony.

It was a small affair, in consideration of the bride's mother's condition. And the groomsman's wife's condition. And the groom's housekeeper's condition. And the vicar's wife's condition.

"Lud, I hope it is not contagious," Marissa whispered to Solicitor Castin's handsome new assistant, who had recently been her deceased husband's handsome valet. Redding, who rocked back in his seat, had agreed with Wynn that a man of affairs was a somewhat less scandalous affair—less scandalous escort, that is—than a mere valet. "Heavens," Marissa continued, "I must be one of the only females in the chapel who is not breeding, except for dear Torrie's spinster aunt Ann. And the bride." She squinted toward the altar, mistrusting that glow her new sister-in-law wore. "I hope."

"You have never looked more beautiful, my love," Wynn murmured to Torrie during Howard's brief sermon.

"I have never been more happy, my love, my husband, my hero."

Lady Duchamp gave birth to twin boys in October. Lord Duchamp was so overjoyed his heart almost burst with pride, but he could not let it. He had to stay around to watch his sons grow into fine men, like his new son-in-law.

That same month, Ruthie and Young Cyrus had a daughter. They named the babe Young Ruth, in the family tradition.

Barrogi and Rosie, in their own wisdom, had named their *bambino* Ace, for luck.

A few months later, Bette Campe, formerly Lady Lynbrook, had a son, and so did the vicar's wife.

Torrie and Wynn's first child was a girl, an exquisite cherub with her father's dark curls and her mother's nose, thank goodness. The ecstatic parents called her Fancine, after one of her grandmothers. And if she arrived in this world precisely nine months from the wedding, well, who was keeping score?

They saved the gold and diamond key for her, hoping that someday it would help little Fanny open her own heart to an everlasting love, just like theirs.

ABOUT THE AUTHOR

The author of more than two dozen Regency romances, **Barbara Metzger** is the proud recipient of two *Romantic Times* Career Achievement Awards for Regencies. When not writing Regencies or reading them, she paints, gardens, volunteers at the local library, and goes beachcombing on the beautiful Long Island shore with her little dog, Hero. She loves to hear from her readers, care of Signet or through her Web site, www.BarbaraMetzger.com.